C

M

Mystery Series

Book 24

Hope Callaghan

hopecallaghan.com

Copyright © 2023
All rights reserved.

This book is a work of fiction. Although places mentioned may be real, the characters, names and incidents, and all other details are products of the author's imagination and are fictitious. Any resemblance to actual organizations, events, or actual persons, living or dead is purely coincidental.

No part of this publication may be copied, reproduced in any format, by any means, electronic or otherwise, without prior consent from the copyright owner and publisher of this book.

Visit my website for new releases and special offers:
hopecallaghan.com

CONTENTS

"Trust in the Lord with all thine heart; and lean not unto thine own understanding. In all thy ways acknowledge him, and he shall direct thy paths." **Proverbs 3:5-6 KJV.**

Chapter 1

Millie slipped into the back, watching as Donovan Sweeney, the ship's purser and her husband, Nic, approached the small stage. Her eyes scanned the room filled with the entertainment staff, searching for her boss, Andy Walker, who had left the ship as soon as it had docked early that morning.

He'd been experiencing some concerning symptoms, including being disoriented. Thankfully, Cat, his newly betrothed, had convinced him to schedule a doctor's appointment.

Millie consulted her watch. It was getting close to departure time, and Andy still hadn't returned. She noticed Danielle standing nearby and made her way over. "Have you heard from Andy?" she whispered.

"Not a peep. I ran into Annette a few minutes ago. Cat texted her that things weren't going well and she wasn't sure if they were going to make it back on board in time."

Millie pressed a hand to her chest. "Not going well."

Nic approached the microphone. "I know how busy everyone is, so we'll make this brief. As many of you already know, Andy has been experiencing some complications regarding his health. Without going into detail and to respect his privacy, he's taking an emergency leave and won't be with us for this week's voyage."

A hushed murmur filled the crowded room.

Nic stepped back, and Donovan took his place. "The show must go on. There's no time to find a replacement. We've requested to have Millie fill in for Andy, something she's done in the past. We have no doubt the entertainment department will run smoothly in Andy's absence. Danielle will fill in as assistant cruise director."

Donovan craned his neck. "Millie, are you here?"

She stepped away from the others and began making her way toward the front of the room.

"There she is." Donovan motioned for her to join them on the stage. "I know I speak for all the staff when I say our thoughts and prayers are with Andy this week. Please do not listen to or start rumors about what might happen. We don't know. What we do know is Andy is in very capable hands and we're hopeful for the best possible outcome. Millie, would you like to say a few words?"

"I-yes. We all love and respect Andy. Nic and I will keep him in our prayers as well. Filling his shoes is a big job. I'll need everyone's help to keep things running smoothly." Millie patted her radio. "I'll keep my radio handy if you need anything."

She wrapped it up with a small pep talk and passed the mic back to Donovan, who added a few words and dismissed the group.

Millie hung back and waited for the room to clear so she could have a private word with Donovan and her husband. Danielle slipped in next to her. "This is scary. Poor Andy."

"It is scary. I wonder if Cat's going to stay behind, too." Millie posed the question as soon as Nic and Donovan were free.

"She's taken a week's leave," Donovan confirmed. "I've already talked to the gift shop's staff and we'll have her shifts covered."

"Do they have any idea what might be wrong with him?" Millie asked.

"It has something to do with his heart," Nic said. "I'm sorry we sprang this on both of you without warning. We finished our conference call with him right before we came down here. The doctors are running some tests. Now all we can do is wait."

"The most important thing to focus on is Andy getting the proper diagnosis and treatment."

"I'll be right by Millie's side," Danielle promised. "We've done it before and we can do it again."

Nic's cell phone rang. He glanced at the screen. "It's corporate. I need to take this call."

Millie thanked them, asking Donovan and Nic to let her know when they had an update, and headed to Andy's office to grab his weekly schedule.

With a few tweaks and rearranging, she was confident the week would be trouble-free except for Santa's Turkey Trot Parade, something new Andy was rolling out for the holiday season.

Determined not to become overwhelmed, she set the file folder with the parade's details off to the side and hustled upstairs for the muster drill and passenger check-in. Millie made her way to her designated area and helped process the passengers assigned to her group.

Finally, the PA announcements of those who hadn't yet completed the mandatory check-in ended as the ship drifted away from the dock and they began their journey to the open sea.

Millie's radio crackled as a call came in from the head of gangway security. "Millie, do you copy?" Suharto's voice echoed over the airwaves.

"I'm here, Suharto."

"I heard Andy will not be with us this week."

"That's correct."

"I will send you the upcoming port gangway schedule. Andy likes to keep a copy on hand."

Millie's cell phone *pinged*. "That was fast."

"We do not mess around. Good luck, Miss Millie."

"Thanks. I'm going to need it." She headed to her first of many trivia contests, followed by a check of the lido deck's sail away party.

Early evening arrived and Danielle radioed, inviting her to join her in the galley for their dinner break.

"There she is," Annette said as she strolled inside. "The busiest woman on board the ship."

"No kidding." Millie let out a low groan as she climbed onto an empty barstool. "The good news is this week will fly by. Has anyone heard from Andy or Cat?"

"Not yet," Danielle said.

"I talked to her earlier. She said to tell you the doctors scheduled some tests for tomorrow, but it will be a few days before they hear anything back." Annette rattled off the name of the hospital. "Andy's symptoms were serious enough for them to admit him."

"Poor Cat and Andy."

"Let me know if there's anything I can do to help this week," Annette said.

"Ditto for me, Miss Millie," Amit chimed in.

"Thanks." Millie patted her stomach. "I'm starving."

"I have a couple RTG, ready-to-go, meals left." Annette ran to the refrigerated shelf, grabbed two bags, and handed them to Danielle and Millie. "Turkey on whole wheat wraps with an organic avocado spread, banana chips, Greek yogurt and mixed nuts."

"I can't eat this. It sounds too healthy," Danielle joked. "Where's the junk food?"

"No junk food for you." Annette playfully wagged her finger. "You need to be at the top of your game."

"Yeah. Yeah." Danielle unwrapped her wrap and took a big bite. "I was kidding. I love the RTG meals. There are too many carbs on the buffet."

They chatted about the cruise itinerary and then the subject shifted back to Andy, with Millie expressing her concern. "I've been praying for them all day. Maybe we can pray together."

"That's a great idea."

The friends joined hands, and Millie bowed her head. "Dear Heavenly Father, thank you for bringing us together. Lord, we lift Andy and Cat up. Please lead the doctors to perform the right tests to figure out what is wrong with our friend. Give them wisdom to make the correct diagnosis. Thank you for your Son, our Savior. Amen."

"Amen," the others echoed.

"And on that note." Danielle crumpled her dinner bag and tossed it in the trash. "It's time to get back out there."

"Thanks for the pep talk and food." Millie headed down to check on the late-night comedy show. She lingered for a few minutes and slipped back out, circling around past the casino bar.

Near midnight, Millie made her final rounds with her last stop at the Tahitian Nights Dance Club. She reached the landing and found the place swarming with security guards.

An ear-piercing scream rang out. It was followed by a loud crash.

Chapter 2

Millie instinctively ducked behind the wall separating the dance club from the main corridor. Shouting ensued, and the few security guards who were standing nearby ran inside.

She crept forward, keeping low as she peered around the corner, past a pair of toppled barstools. A woman flailed wildly, surrounded by security guards on each side.

"I want to see the captain of this ship this very minute!" she shouted. "How dare you treat me like a criminal? Do you have any idea who I am?"

Two women hovered nearby, attempting to calm the woman, which only seemed to infuriate her.

"This is physical and verbal harassment."

One woman leaned in and whispered in her ear, which seemed to calm her slightly, signaling to Millie it was safe to approach. "What is going on?"

The bartender's hand trembled as she motioned to the woman. "The passenger ordered a drink. She was with a man. I don't see him now. They started arguing, and he left. She took a taste of her drink and started swearing at me, telling me it was terrible. I tried to take it from her and she threw it at me."

"You started arguing with me." The tall, thin blonde's eyes sparked with anger as she jabbed her finger at the employee. "I'll have you fired. I'll have all of you fired."

"Harper," the woman at her side soothed. "I'm sure it was a misunderstanding. You don't want to cause a scene, not now."

"They're not going to get away with treating me disrespectfully." Harper jerked her arm, struggling to free herself. "Where's Bryce?"

"He left." The second woman leaned in. "It's been a long day. Let's head back to the cabin."

Millie surveyed the damages. "The surveillance camera footage will help determine exactly what happened."

Harper spun around, focusing her wrath on Millie. "Who are you?"

"Millie Armati, the ship's cruise director."

The woman snarled. "You're a pathetic excuse for a cruise director. I've never seen such a lame lineup of activities in my life."

Millie could feel the tips of her ears burn as their eyes met. The woman's pupils were dilated, and she immediately suspected she was under the influence of some sort of drug. "I think it's best if you and your companions return to your cabin for the remainder of the evening. Our security staff will accompany you."

The woman standing closest to Harper reached for her arm. "Let's call it a night. I'm sure Bryce is back in the cabin."

The woman's eyes narrowed. She muttered unintelligibly under her breath, but thankfully began moving toward the exit.

Two of the ship's security guards followed behind, and Millie motioned for the third guard, who stood off to the side. "Something tells me this isn't the end."

"I'm going to contact Dave Patterson to fill him in and request that he station someone outside their cabin for the rest of the evening."

Millie stayed behind to help clean up. All the while, the young bartender insisted she had done nothing to set the woman off. "She started fighting with the man she came in with. I could tell she was getting very angry."

"Was security around when it first happened?"

The bartender nodded. “By the doorway. Her voice, she kept raising it. I handed her the drink, and she started complaining about it. She kept asking me, do you have any idea who I am? She said it over and over.”

Millie ran a damp rag over the bar top. “Is there any way to pull up the passenger’s full name?”

“Yes.” The bartender tapped the order screen. “Her name is Harper Rothshield.”

“Harper Rothshield,” Millie repeated. “Do you know what she and the man were arguing about?”

“A woman he was flirting with.”

“Booze and bad relationships are never a good combination.” Millie sighed. “I hate to say it, but something tells me we might need to keep an eye on this group.”

With the bar back in order, Millie headed home. The bridge was quiet and the only sound was the faint hum of the navigational equipment. The lights were dimmed, and it took a minute for her eyes to adjust. She found her husband near the outboard bridge wing, chatting with Dave Patterson.

Patterson noticed her first. "Hello, Millie. Were your ears burning? We were talking about you."

"Nope, although they were burning earlier when a passenger decided to start causing trouble up in the nightclub and called me a pathetic cruise director."

"Harper Rothshield," Patterson said. "I was filling Nic in. According to one of the women who is traveling with her, she's gone off her medication and picked a fight with her boyfriend."

"Hopefully, it's an isolated incident and the rest of the cruise will be smooth sailing."

"It's possible, but I wouldn't hold my breath. Harper Rothshield is a former reality television star."

"Great," Millie groaned. "She threatened to have me fired."

"She doesn't have that sort of pull, but she could make our lives unpleasant for the duration of our voyage. At the very least, there's the distinct possibility she'll be one of our higher maintenance passengers," Nic said. "We'll see what tomorrow brings. There is one more tidbit of information we found out while talking with Ms. Rothshield's companions."

Patterson picked up. "She was in a rehab program, somewhere out in Arizona. One of those ritzy, glitzy ones. She checked out midway through, insisting they weren't helping her and that she needed a break. She, along with her boyfriend and two other women booked this cruise last minute."

Millie briefly closed her eyes. "Thanks for the heads up. I guess our plan is to hope for the best and prepare for the worst."

"Exactly."

"I have another half an hour on the bridge," Nic said. "I'll see you at home in a few."

Millie trekked down the hall leading to the apartment. Scout, their small pup, met her at the door and promptly pounced on her shoe. "You're a sight for sore eyes." She scooped him up and carried him out onto the balcony.

The clear skies were filled with twinkling stars for as far as the eye could see. Her thoughts turned to Andy and Cat, and she said a small prayer for her friends.

Tomorrow's sea day would be jam-packed with activities. Adding Andy's job to her plate was a curveball she wasn't expecting, but was determined to handle. A potentially problematic passenger added one more layer of stress. Perhaps the reality star's meltdown was an isolated incident and when the woman calmed down she would realize that her behavior at the club would not be tolerated.

If not, something told Millie it was going to be a very long week.

*****

Millie was up early the next morning and hit the ground running, leaving Nic behind in their apartment since a sea day meant his schedule was a little less structured.

The Sunrise Stride was the first activity on her long list. She reached the jogging track and greeted several passengers who were already circling around.

The balmy sea air was the perfect start to a busy day and by the time Millie finished the two-mile trek, the sun was peeking over the horizon. She took it as a sign that it would be an "I-can-handle-whatever-is-thrown-at-me-day."

Millie swung by the crewmember's dining room for a quick bite to eat and caught up with Danielle to go over the revised entertainment schedule.

"I heard about the nightclub nuisance who was tearing the place apart last night."

"The woman was off the charts." Millie rolled her eyes. "She was threatening me, threatening the security team. I hope it's a simple case of her not taking her meds and now she's back on them."

"Do you remember her name so I can be on the lookout for her?"

"Harper Rothshield."

Danielle made a choking sound. "Seriously?"

"Yeah. I take it you've heard of her?"

"She was in some reality television show. Thirty Days to Evade or something like that. She partnered with a guy. Actually, I think they were a couple. I watched it for a while until she started doing some crazy stuff."

"Do you remember the guy's name?"

Danielle rubbed her chin. "Bryce. He was a nice-looking guy, kind of mellow. I never could figure out what he saw in her."

"Bryce." Millie toyed with her straw. "His name was mentioned last night. I think he may also be on board."

"The guy is here?" Danielle asked. "I can't believe he's still with her."

Millie's activity app chimed, and she sprang to her feet. "Time to roll. I'll catch up with you later."

The morning passed without incident, and there was no sign of the troubled passenger. She reached the cozy seating area across from the casino and began assembling the supplies for the "All About Jamaica" afternoon trivia, a port which hadn't been a part of Siren of the Seas' itinerary for several years, not since Millie first joined the cruise line.

"Mill-ee." Felix sashayed toward her. "How's my bestie?"

"Stress-dee," Millie laughed. "How are you?"

"Fantastic. What could be better than co-hosting trivia with you?" Felix clapped his hands. "I was thinking we could improvise this round, spice things up and make it more of a charades-type trivia."

"Charades?"

"You ask the question. I act out the answers. Jamaica is one of my absolute fave ports. The people are so warm and friendly." Felix added an accent. "If I ever quit working and move to an island, I want to be a Jamaican islander."

Millie grinned. "Tell me something I didn't know."

"I thought you'd never ask. Let me act it out." Felix pumped his arms and jogged in place. "Jamaica is famous for this."

"Exercise," Millie guessed.

"No, silly." Felix slapped his forehead. "Jamaicans are the fastest runners on earth."

"Cool. I didn't know that."

"Here's another fun fact." Felix pressed his palms together and closed his eyes.

"They like to meditate."

His eyes flew open. "You're not very good at charades, are you?" he teased.

“Not at all.”

“Jamaica has more churches per square mile than any other country.”

“Ah. Very interesting.” Millie grabbed a handful of pencils. “This is fun. Give me one more.”

“I hoped you would be on board to trivia things up.” Felix reached into his backpack, pulled out a black, yellow and red beanie and stuck it on his head. He placed a hand on his hip and sashayed in a circle.

“I don’t have a clue,” Millie chuckled.

“Reggae,” Felix admonished. “Jamaica is the home of reggae music.”

“You sold me. If nothing else, you’re totally entertaining.” She gave him a thumbs up. “Charade trivia it is.”

A large group gathered, and Millie and Felix played off each other with Felix acting, and Millie hosting. They drew a large crowd who stopped to see them in action.

The trivia ended and a spontaneous round of applause ensued. Felix, his face beaming, took a bow. He fielded several questions, most about when he planned to host another special round of trivia.

Finally, the crowd cleared and Felix helped Millie finish cleaning up. "We've done Jamaica. I have another idea for char-trivia."

His app dinged. "It'll have to wait. Time to run. Toodles."

"Toodles to you too." Millie locked the supply cabinet and turned to go when she heard someone call her name.

"Millie Armati."

She pivoted, her heart plummeting when she spotted Harper Rothshield marching toward her.

Chapter 3

Harper Rothshield blocked Millie's path. "Millie Armati."

"Hello, Ms. Rothshield," she coolly replied. "How are you feeling today?"

"I'm feeling fine. I was feeling fine last night when the ship's overzealous security guards caused a scene. You embarrassed me and my friends half to death."

Millie bit back a snarky reply and silently counted to ten. "I'm sorry if there was any misunderstanding on our part."

Harper placed her hands on her hips. "My friends said you seemed awfully interested in who I am and then made a big deal about making sure I returned to my cabin."

“I…” Millie blinked rapidly. “My job is to help ensure the safety of passengers, including those who exhibit unacceptable behavior.”

“Unacceptable behavior,” the woman sputtered. “This ship’s staff was the one exhibiting unacceptable behavior. The incompetent bartender spilled my drink. I tried to get out of the way, tripped on the tippy barstools and then I got blamed for what happened.”

“The staff and passengers have a different version of what took place.”

“Are you calling me a liar?” Harper’s voice rose an octave. “I believe you are. No one accuses me of lying. You’re going to be sorry we ever crossed paths.” The woman’s threat hung in the air as she stormed off.

She reached the end of the corridor and swung back around. Her lips were moving and although Millie couldn’t hear what she was saying, something told her the troublesome passenger intended to make good on her threat.

"I..." Millie started to follow after her and wisely changed her mind. Instead, she headed down to the security office. She gave the door a light rap and stuck her head around the corner where she found Dave Patterson seated at his desk.

He motioned Millie inside. "Hey, Millie. How's it going?"

"Great. So far, so good, except for Harper Rothshield, who confronted me and tried to cause a scene...again."

Patterson leaned back in his chair and folded his arms. "The woman is making her rounds. She was down here insisting I issue a letter of apology for last night's incident."

"She claims the bartender spilled her drink. She tried to get out of the way, tripped on a tippy barstool, and security was called," Millie said. "There was no mention of an argument with the guy she was with."

"Bryce Bridges. I heard the same version—from her, but a different version from the staff and other passengers who witnessed what happened. She started arguing with a female passenger at the bar. The woman walked away. Harper took a sip of her drink, started complaining about it, and threw it at our bartender, Eliza. Eliza called security, and that's when Rothshield caused a scene."

"Why don't you write the letter and let it go?"

"Because none of the staff or crew was to blame, not to mention she could use it against us." Patterson slipped his reading glasses on and grabbed the sheet of paper sitting on his desk. "Kimberly Frye, a passenger who is traveling with Rothshield, stated the woman may have stopped taking her medication. Throw in an abundance of alcohol from a woman who walked away from a swanky rehab center last week, toss in a male companion who was showing interest in another female passenger late at night and it spells trouble."

"She's still very upset and told me I was going to be sorry."

"What we have is an unstable passenger who is trying to throw her weight around. If we cave now and give in to her demands, I'm afraid it will only be the tip of the iceberg." Patterson suggested they try to avoid all direct contact with the woman, giving her time to cool off. "We're stopping in Jamaica tomorrow. Perhaps she and her friends plan to spend some time ashore…"

"And not get back on board," Millie joked. "We can only hope." She thanked Patterson for the update and headed back out.

Hours later, she returned home, exhausted from her non-stop schedule. She made quick work of getting ready for bed, and as soon as Millie's head hit the pillow, she was out.

*****

Scout followed Nic out of the bedroom early the next morning, his tail low and his ears drooping as he watched him leave.

"Poor Scout." Millie scooped him up. "It was a long day yesterday with you cooped up inside. How about you go with me to see passengers off the ship?"

Scout's ears perked up, and Millie knew she had his attention. "Would you like to go for a ride?"

The pup knew what that meant. He wiggled and squirmed until Millie set him back down. He promptly trotted to the closet door, where his stroller was kept.

"I need to get dressed first." She ran upstairs to get ready and when she returned, she found the pup still parked in front of the closet door, patiently waiting for her to open it.

"We're ready to roll." Millie steered the stroller toward the door and watched as the pup promptly jumped inside.

They reached the exit only minutes to spare before the ship received clearance. The gangway lowered and passengers began exiting.

Millie grabbed the intercom. "Good morning, ladies and gentlemen. This is your cruise director, Millie Armati. We've received clearance, so if you're planning on heading to shore, feel free to make your way down to deck two. It's going to be a beautiful day in Jamaica. Don't forget the sunscreen. Scout and I will be waiting to see you out."

She signed off, and the long lines grew as Millie, with her trusty sidekick by her side, fielded questions and offered suggestions. Finally, the crowds thinned.

"Hey, Millie. Do you copy?"

Millie unclipped her radio and stepped off to the side. "Go ahead, Annette."

"Who's in charge of hosting The Vine luncheon for the sixties cruisers?"

“Luncheon at The Vine?” Millie tapped her scheduler app and sighed. “Me. I completely missed it. I’m on my way, right after I drop Scout off at home.”

Scout wasn’t the least bit happy to discover his outing was being cut short. “I have to head to The Vines. I’ll come back for you later,” she promised.

She reached the specialty restaurant and found Annette waiting for her near the entrance. “We have a few minutes before the guests arrive. Andy typically gives them a gift.”

“I don’t have a gift.” Millie could feel panic start to set in. It was becoming clear she was in over her head, as in way over her head. “Who is this group?”

“The sixties cruisers. They cruise every year around Thanksgiving.” Annette propelled her to the table near the door. “Amit whipped up something special. I hope this will work.”

Stacked in a perfectly formed swirl were elegant black boxes with red ribbons tied around each one. "The table is beautiful."

"Thanks." Annette plucked a box from the top and handed it to Millie. "I'm thinking about promoting Amit to head of Celebrations and special events. He has a knack for creating some knockout goodies."

"He does have a creative flair." Millie carefully untied the ribbon and removed the box's lid. Inside was an orange and gold frosted cupcake with a chocolate leaf tucked into the top. Patterned leaves circled the base. "This is gorgeous."

"It tastes as good as it looks." Annette broke off the tip of the leaf and nibbled the edge. "The cupcake's wrapper is also edible. Try a bite."

Millie plucked the patterned leaf out and sampled the corner. "It is delicious. Let me guess...there's a cream cheese surprise center."

"Yes, and there's a hint of orange in the frosting."

“The guests are going to love them.” Millie polished off the rest of the treat. “Thank you for saving me.”

“You’re welcome. You should see the Christmas reindeer Amit’s working on for the upcoming craft event.”

“He’s helping me host,” Millie said. “I’m sure it will be perfect.”

Guests began arriving, and Millie stood near the door, collecting invitations and greeting them. Thankfully, the group’s leader handled the introductions and speech while she made her rounds, making sure the event ran smoothly.

Several guests lingered after it ended, thanking Annette, Amit, and Millie. “Those cupcakes are simply adorable,” one woman gushed. “I would love a copy of the recipe.”

“I will share it with you.” Amit beamed as he jotted down her cabin number, promising to drop a copy off later that day.

Finally, the last guest departed, and Millie stayed behind to help clean up. With plenty of leftovers, the trio gathered at an empty table near the door to sample the dishes. "I love Thanksgiving. It's all about the food."

"Turkey, gravy, mashed potatoes, stuffing." Annette smacked her lips. "What's not to love?"

Millie thanked them again and made her way topside to host a mini golf competition. As the day wore on, passengers began returning to the ship. She worked her way from top to bottom, forward to aft, checking on events and handling several minor issues.

She popped into the theater to check on bingo and then swung by the apartment to grab Scout. The back on board deadline came and went and when the ship remained docked, Millie ran downstairs to find out what was going on.

"We are missing two passengers," Suharto explained. "They are on their way back now. We'll be leaving shortly."

Millie stood near the gangway and glimpsed movement off in the distance. She watched as a couple sauntered through the gate, moving at a leisurely pace without a worry in the world.

Baoooooommmmmm.

The ship's horn blasted, and Millie stumbled back, clutching her chest.

She wasn't the only one startled by the loud horn. The wayward couple picked up the pace. One of the staff captains and a security guard met them and escorted them the rest of the way.

Millie was the first to greet them as they dinged their keycards. "We've been waiting for you."

"I...we completely lost track of time." The woman pressed a hand to her flushed cheeks. "We were wondering why we were the only ones coming back through the checkpoint."

Millie tapped the top of her watch. "You may want to check to make sure you're on ship's time."

The woman glanced at her watch. "Oh my gosh. You're right. I'm on central time. I'll change it right now."

The couple disappeared into the elevator, and Suharto gave a thumbs up, his signal all passengers were back on board. Millie, curious to find out if Harper had gotten off, waited until the crew finished departure preparations and made her way over. "I was wondering if Harper Rothshield exited the ship today."

"The name sounds familiar," Suharto said.

"She caused some problems in the nightclub last night, and I suspect the woman might be high maintenance during this voyage."

"I will see." Suharto tapped the screen, his eyes narrowing. "Do you know how to spell her name?"

"R-O-T-H-S-H-I-E-L-D," Millie said. "At least I think that's how you spell it."

"She did not get off the ship today."

“There are two other women and a man with her. Do you know if they got off?”

“I will see if their names are linked.” Suharto grew quiet. “Yes. Kimberly Frye and Sierra Geldman, who are in a cabin next to Ms. Rothshield, exited the ship. Bryce Bridges, her cabinmate, also left the ship. All three returned at the same time.”

“I see.” Millie thanked him and mulled over the information on her way back home to return Scout to their apartment.

Why had Rothshield’s friends gotten off yet she remained on board? It was possible she wasn’t feeling well. Or maybe she was working on getting Millie fired. Either way, the fact she hadn’t run into the woman was a positive sign.

Evening was in full swing, and there was a buzz as passengers gathered at the various venues for a pre-dinner snack or cocktail and to enjoy the live music. Tonight’s theater headliner show featured the ship’s singers and dancers, and Millie popped in to check on them before heading to the first of two past guest parties.

Danielle caught up with her and made her way to the other entrance, collecting invitations and welcoming the past guests. The ship's captains arrived for their speech, for the awards presentation and then the band began playing as the guests hit the dance floor.

Millie made her rounds, chatting with the VIPs, inquiring about their day ashore and fielding questions about Andy.

Halfway through, she received a text from Nic, who had left right after his speech, asking her to return to the bridge.

She arrived to find a somber Dave Patterson, Suharto, Donovan Sweeney and Nic gathered at the conference table.

Nic caught her eye and motioned her to join them. "We have a troubling situation. It appears a passenger has gone missing."

Chapter 4

Millie's brows furrowed. "A passenger is missing?"

"It's Harper Rothshield, the woman who was causing trouble in the nightclub," Patterson said. "Bryce Bridges, her boyfriend, is unable to locate her. He also said some of her things were missing from the cabin, including clothes and toiletries. He's tried reaching her via cell phone. We've tried contacting her. Security has searched the ship. There's no sign of her."

"She never left the ship." Millie motioned to Suharto. "You told me earlier that she never got off. The other two women who are traveling with her and Mr. Bridges left, but Harper Rothshield remained on board."

"She's gone now," Donovan said grimly.

Millie pressed a hand to her chest, her mind whirling. "The ship's surveillance cameras—you don't think she went overboard, do you?"

"We're going over them now. Our next step is to page her to see if she responds," Nic said. "It's possible she's injured and we haven't found her yet, which is why you're here. You're all over this ship. Did you happen to run into her today?"

Millie shook her head.

Nic and Patterson exchanged a glance. "Ms. Rothshield was upset over an exchange you two had yesterday afternoon."

"Yes, and I mentioned it right after it happened. We crossed paths when I was finishing up karaoke," Millie said. "She approached me. I tried to smooth things over. She seemed to want to argue."

"From what we were told by her friends, she claims you called her a liar."

"I told her the staff and passengers who were there when the incident at the nightclub occurred had a different version of what took place."

"Regardless of how the conversation went, her companions told us she was very upset with you," Donovan said. "And now she's missing."

"There's one more thing," Nic said. "Harper was taking some strong prescription drugs and planned to quit everything cold turkey."

"Until she went to the nightclub and started drinking. That's a good way to quit cold turkey." Millie briefly closed her eyes, the woman's threat ringing in her ears. "She said I would be sorry. I guess she's making good on her threat."

"We need to find her." Patterson headed toward the door. "If we haven't tracked her down in the next thirty minutes, I'll try paging her on the PA system. I've also arranged a security staff meeting and will distribute photos of her so that everyone on board can keep an eye out for her."

Millie was only steps behind. "She has to be somewhere on board. If the woman planned to jump off the ship, she wouldn't pack clothes. There are hundreds of hiding places, crew areas, security areas, corridor shortcuts, empty conference rooms."

"Making it difficult to find her if she wants to hide," Nic pointed out.

"Maybe she's reliving her days of being on a reality television show," Millie said.

"On board our ship," Patterson gloomily replied.

Millie returned to her scheduled activities and, as promised, the announcements for Harper to report to guest services ensued. They continued intermittently for several hours before stopping, and she was hopeful the woman had finally been located.

She ran into Danielle on an upper deck. "I heard the announcement for Harper Rothshield. She's missing?"

"Is or was." Millie briefly filled her in. "She was ticked at me, packed her things and went into hiding while her friends were onshore in Jamaica."

Danielle let out a low whistle. "And you say she went off her meds?"

"And skipped out of her rehab center."

"Talk about cruising cold turkey. If I was going to do something like that, I'm not sure I would do it on board a cruise ship."

"The announcements have stopped. Hopefully, security tracked her down." Millie asked Danielle to keep an eye out for her before heading to the stage to wrap up the headliner show.

After finishing, she slipped into Andy's office and settled in behind the desk.

Footsteps echoed and Millie glanced up to find Felix and Alison Coulter, another of the ship's dancers, standing in the doorway.

“Felix and I thought we saw lights on. You look stressed. Is there anything we can do to help?”

Millie slid her chair back. “I was going over Andy’s schedule. Santa’s Turkey Trot Parade is tomorrow.”

“Andy’s been ironing out the details for weeks now. It should be a blast.” Felix rubbed his hands together. “I haven’t made a final decision, but I’m leaning toward dressing up as a jester.”

“I’ll be one of the Thanksgiving parade elves,” Alison said.

“And I’m going to be ready for a straitjacket,” Millie joked. “I’ve never hosted a parade. Unfortunately, all the little details are still in Andy’s head. We can’t even do a dry run to make sure the kinks are worked out.”

“He kept notes,” Felix said. “He has a file folder around here somewhere.”

“I have it.” Millie motioned to the open manila file folder on the desk. “His detailed instructions read like major surgery.”

“But Andy did the pre-planning before he left,” Alison said. “We can wing it. If we make a mistake, we’ll just keep plugging along. I’m sure no one will even notice.”

“Practice makes perfect,” Felix quipped. “The staff and crew have their marching orders. All we have to do is put the parade in motion.”

“I wish I felt even the teensiest bit optimistic this won’t be a dumpster fire,” Millie moaned.

Felix patted her shoulder. “It’s going to be fine. Have a little faith in yourself.”

After they left, Millie gathered up Andy’s parade notes and thought about Harper Rothshield. They’d stopped calling her name hours ago. Thinking there was at least a sliver of a silver lining to her day and the woman had been located, she called down to security.

Oscar, Patterson's right-hand man, picked up. "Hello, Millie."

"Hey, Oscar. I'm sure Patterson has clocked out for the day."

"He has."

"The reason I'm calling is to inquire about whether the missing passenger, Harper Rothshield, has been located."

"No. We have not found her and are still looking. We are reviewing the surveillance camera recordings a second time." Oscar told her they'd confirmed the woman had not exited the ship. "We are hopeful she can be found."

"This is terrible." Passengers occasionally went missing, but only for a few short hours, not a full day. The fact the woman had packed some clothes and then vanished was concerning. Perhaps she had figured out a way to get off the ship without passing through security. Millie wished him luck and headed home.

Nic wasn't on the bridge, and she found him and Scout out on the balcony.

"Hey."

Nic shifted to the side to make room for his wife. "How many more days do we have left of this voyage?"

"Too many," Millie sighed. "I called down to security a few minutes ago. There's still no sign of Harper Rothshield."

"We're waiting for the full twenty-four hours before contacting the authorities, although there's not much they can do considering we're in the middle of the ocean."

"Has security spoken with her friends and boyfriend again?"

"At length," Nic said. "They're as puzzled as we are. She's still not answering her phone. Patterson has a call in to see if he can get a trace on it. Unfortunately, as you know those things take time."

"The fact she went off her meds is concerning," Millie said. "She struck me as slightly unstable, which could be a bad sign."

"Very bad."

Millie rummaged around in the fridge and assembled a shared plate of fresh fruit, meat, and cheese slices. The couple dined on the balcony, going over the following day's schedule before turning in.

She spent a restless night worrying about Andy and wondering if Harper had been found.

Millie woke early the next morning and slipped out of bed. Nic caught up with her in the kitchen a short time later. "I spoke to Patterson. They still haven't located our missing passenger. The countdown has begun before we'll need to report it."

"You don't think..." Millie's voice trailed off.

"That the boyfriend is lying? That he did something to Harper and is trying to cover by

claiming she took some things from the cabin?"
Nic's jaw tightened. "We're not ruling anything out."

"I hope that's not the case." Millie left not long after Nic and flew through her morning routine, wrapping it up by hosting a staff meeting to go over the parade route.
After finishing, she grabbed a cup of tea, meandering past the aft pool when she noticed the cleaning crew, along with the maintenance crew, standing next to it.

Changing direction, Millie circled around, curious to find out exactly what they were doing. "Hey, guys." She leaned over the side and noticed something bright red sitting at the bottom of the pool. "What in the world?"

Chapter 5

Frank Bauer, the head of maintenance, grabbed his radio. "Hey, Sharky. You there?"

"I'm here. What's up, Frank?"

"I need you to bring the portable pump to the deck eleven aft pool. If the second one is still working, bring that one too."

"You want me to bring the pumps to the pool?" Sharky asked.

"10-4."

"Ohhh-kay. I'm on my way."

Frank began motioning to the crew. "We need to secure the area to keep guests away while we drain the pool and try to get this thing out."

Millie studied the tear in the pool cover and the bright red mobility scooter lying at the bottom. "Why not just hook something to it and pull it out?"

"Those scooters take two twelve-volt batteries. Depending on how long it's been down there, the acid could be leaching into the water." Frank and his crew began unstrapping the ripped cover. "We'll have to drain it, get the scooter out, clean the pool, and then refill it. I'm thinking this is gonna take most of the day."

As promised, Sharky showed up with a cartful of equipment a short time later. "What's going on?"

"This." Frank led him to the pool's edge.

He let out a low whistle. "Let me guess...one of our passengers was out drinking and driving and accidentally drove into the pool."

"Could be. The cleaning crew found it this morning. I've already contacted security. They're checking the videos to find out exactly what happened. There's no ship's sticker on it, so I'm guessing it belongs to a passenger."

"I'll find out if anyone has reported one missing." Millie stepped away to make a call to the first place she could think of.

"Guest services. Nikki Tan speaking."

"Hey, Nikki. Millie here. Has anyone reported a missing mobility scooter?"

"Let me check."

Millie could hear rustling on the other end of the line.

Nikki returned. "As a matter of fact, we had one reported missing about an hour ago. It was a passenger in cabin 11313. It's red and has a yellow reflective strip across the back of the seat."

Millie circled around to the back side of the submerged scooter, taking note of the yellow strip. "It's up here frolicking around in the aft lido deck pool."

"Huh?"

"The missing scooter is in the bottom of the pool," Millie said bluntly. "Maintenance is here, draining the pool and working on getting it out."

"You're kidding."

"Nope. We'll need to find out if we have any extra scooters available to loan the passenger while we try to get this one up and running again." Millie's gaze lifted to the surveillance cameras. "Before you contact the passenger, let me get with Patterson. It's possible the passenger is behind the incident."

"No problem. Let me know if I need to do anything on my end. In the meantime, I'll see if I can track down a spare scooter."

She thanked Nikki and stood watching as Sharky assembled the pumps and began draining the water. He had a brief word with Frank Bauer and joined Millie, who was snapping pictures of the damaged cover and water-logged scooter.

"What kind of nutjob would drive their scooter—or any scooter for that matter—into a pool?"

"I have no idea. I'll need to start doing some rearranging now that the pool area will be closed for most of the day." Millie motioned toward the cabin area. "I called down to guest services and spoke with Nikki Tan. She confirmed a passenger who is booked in a spa suite reported the scooter missing."

Sharky made a choking sound. "Someone stole a passenger's scooter, took it for a joyride and drove it into the pool?"

"It's looking that way. I guess you'll be up here until you can get it out and refill the pool with uncontaminated water."

"Yeah. Without even checking, I can tell you the batteries are toast. I have a coupla old ones from my Flamethrower. Depending on the condition of the scooter, we might be able to dry it and pop in the replacements. Either that, or see if there's an extra scooter on board that's not being used."

"Nikki's already looking into it." Millie wished him luck and trekked down to the security office.

She found the office door locked and the lights off. Millie began backtracking and made it halfway down the hall when Patterson barreled around the corner, heading in her direction. She waited for him to catch up. "Have you talked to the maintenance crew up on the pool deck?"

"I just left there. Sharky said I just missed you. A passenger's scooter is sitting at the bottom of the pool. I'm on my way to my office to see if I can figure out exactly what happened."

"I have a few minutes to spare." Millie fell into step. "I wouldn't mind seeing what the cameras caught."

"The more, the merrier." Patterson unlocked the door and pulled a chair around for Millie before logging into the surveillance system and accessing the aft lido deck's camera recordings.

She grew quiet as they watched the evening cleaning crew cover the pool around eleven p.m., a routine task and safety precaution to deter passengers from accessing the pool after hours.

Patterson paused the recording and began jotting notes on a yellow pad. "The safety crew installed the cover."

"I'm sure when you were up there, you noticed the sizeable rip in it, large enough to sink a scooter," Millie said. "Either the person cut a hole in it or the weight of the scooter ripped it and it fell in."

"I'm going to go with it ripped from the weight. We'll find out soon enough." Patterson hit the play button.

At four-ten that morning, the red scooter, driven by a hooded figure, appeared. The grainy image showed them skirting the edge of the bar area. They disappeared and then reappeared on the opposite end. Around and around they went, all the while studying the pool.

“They’re trying to figure out how to access the pool,” Patterson said.

“In other words, casing the joint,” Millie said. “I was thinking the same thing.”

After the third trip around, the driver steered the scooter up the tiled incline. They paused near the top and glanced over their shoulder. In a flash, the scooter flew forward, becoming almost airborne.

It landed hard on top of the cover. The cover dipped down and violently bounced back up.

The hooded driver scrambled out of the seat and leapt over the edge, landing lightly on the deck.

“The scooter’s driver is interestingly agile...agile enough to abandon the scooter and sprint to safety,” Millie pointed out.

“You’re right.” Patterson replayed the video, starting at the point where the scooter first appeared. “They’re intentionally scoping out the pool and hiding their face behind the hoodie.”

"Yep."

After the perpetrator landed on the deck, they stood watching as the scooter continued bouncing. It slowly sank while the cover collapsed under the weight. The scooter teetered back and forth and then disappeared.

The hooded driver thrust their hand in the air in a "V" victory signal and ran off, heading in the direction they'd come from.

"It appears to be an intentional act of vandalism by either a crewmember or a passenger." Patterson blew air through thinned lips. "It appears I have my work cut out for me."

"You and me both." Millie headed for the door and abruptly stopped. "Has Harper Rothshield surfaced?"

Patterson shook his head. "She sent a random text to Kimberly Frye, one of the women she's traveling with, something about not worrying about her. She was fine and hanging out with some new friends."

Millie arched a brow. "That's odd. What about the boyfriend?"

"He hasn't been able to add much, other than to tell us Harper has disappeared before."

"It's possible he's behind her disappearance."

"I'm not ruling anything out." Patterson's jaw tightened. "He could have her phone and is the one sending the texts."

"Maybe you should search their cabin."

"We already have. He's cooperated and allowed us full access," Patterson said. "The other women who boarded with them made a similar comment about how Harper has gone off her medication before and exhibited erratic behavior."

Millie twirled her finger near her forehead. "I think the woman might need some serious help."

"Serious professional help." Patterson grimaced. "But first we have to find her."

"How much do you know about the friends?"

"Kimberly Frye, who also happens to be Bryce's sister, lives in Florida. Sierra Geldman is the second woman traveling with Rothshield. She's from Atlanta."

"And where are Rothshield and Bryce Bridges from?" Millie asked.

"New York."

"New York." Millie eyed the papers on Patterson's desk. "What else do you know about them?"

"All are roughly the same age. Geldman and Frye are staying in the cabin next door. I believe they're all single. They attended one of the singles' get-togethers when they first boarded," Patterson said. "At least that's what they told me."

"Interesting." Millie wished him luck and made a beeline for Andy's office to revise the activities involving the aft pool. She printed the schedule, ran down to guest services to make copies, and then delivered them to the housekeeping department so the room stewards could distribute the printed updates.

Millie uploaded the revised version for the passengers' apps and headed to her first official activity.

The morning flew by, and as the hours passed, her anxiety over the upcoming parade grew.

Near noon, she returned to the lido deck's aft pool to check on the scooter's removal and recovery project.

She found Sharky at the bottom of the empty pool, an open toolbox at his side. "I finished disengaging the driving mechanism and wheels." He wrapped ropes around the back of the scooter and tested the knots by giving them a firm tug.

“We’re going to do this nice and easy,” he said. “Start pulling.”

A small group of maintenance workers began pulling on the ropes, moving the scooter toward the edge of the pool while Sharky guided it along. “We’ll have to put more manpower behind it to get this thing up and over.”

Additional crewmembers arrived and Millie held her breath as the scooter crept up the side of the pool.

“Easy…easy,” Sharky said. “We’re almost there.”

The scooter made it up and over the edge, and a spontaneous round of applause ensued.

Sharky scrambled up the side steps and high-fived his guys. “Good job. Now we gotta see what condition it’s in.” He steered it forward. “The good news is there are no visible signs of damage.”

He grabbed a screwdriver and began removing the battery cover. Water gushed out. “The batteries are toast. The wiring looks okay. If we can get this thing cleaned up, dried out and new batteries installed, I think we'll be back in business."

Millie watched as Sharky maneuvered the scooter off to the side. "How are you going to get this thing downstairs?"

"I'm glad you asked." Sharky patted the seat. "Can you keep an eye on it? I'll be back in five."

"Sure."

Sharky gave Millie the once-over.

"What are you doing?"

"Trying to figure out how much you weigh."

"You should never ask a woman how much she weighs," Millie joked.

"I'm gonna guess around one twenty-five."

"Close. The last time I stepped on a scale, I was at one thirty. The holidays are never my friend."

"Cool. I think that'll work."

"Work for what?"

“I’ll fill you in when I get back.” Sharky snapped the lid on his toolbox and hurried off.

While she waited, Millie studied her schedule, her eyes drawn to Santa’s Turkey Trot Parade. Andy had cleared his schedule from two o’clock on and all she found was “parade,” which meant she would also need to spend most of her afternoon preparing for the big event.

A sick feeling settled in the pit of her stomach. She knew absolutely nothing about coordinating an event of that magnitude. Yes, she’d been involved here and there, adding her input as her boss planned the route and ironed out the details, but Andy had been the go-to.

A flash of black caught Millie’s eye.

The maintenance workers dove for cover as the flash careened around the corner and came to a screeching halt in front of Millie. It was Sharky, seated atop the Flamethrower, his customized souped-up hotrod scooter, grinning from ear to ear. He wasn’t alone.

Chapter 6

Sharky's cat, Fin, slinked to the opposite side of the scooter's basket and nudged Millie's hand.

"Look at you?" she cooed, scratching his ears. "You're one brave little kitty for letting Sharky cart you all over this ship, driving like a maniac."

"Me driving like a maniac? Crazy people who drive scooters into pools are the ones you need to watch out for." Sharky slipped the other end of the rope he'd used to extricate the scooter from the pool through the hook on the Flamethrower's back bumper. "You got a few extra minutes to give me a hand?"

"Maybe." Millie's brows furrowed. "What sort of hand?"

"I'm towing this beauty downstairs and someone has to steer it."

"That's why you wanted to know how much I weighed. Why don't you load it on a cart and push it downstairs?"

"Because the wheelbase is too wide for the smaller carts, and the larger ones are all being used. I need someone lightweight, plus I don't trust any of these dufuses." Sharky jerked his thumb toward the men who were in the process of folding the damaged pool cover. "The last time I left them alone with the Flamethrower, they stuck a banana in my tailpipe."

Millie grinned, remembering the incident and how it had scared Sharky half to death. His concerns were valid. "I'll do it, but only if you promise to drive at a safe speed. We'll be navigating through some crowded deck areas."

"Not a problem. The extra weight and towing are gonna put a drain on my battery. We'll be lucky if we're able to mosey along at a snail's pace."

"I suppose." Millie reluctantly climbed onto the scooter and, as soon as she sat, she realized she'd made a big mistake. Her bottom was instantly both wet and cold. “Great.”

Sharky grabbed a towel from the Flamethrower’s storage compartment and handed it to her. “The seat is soaking wet.”

“Now you tell me.” Millie folded the towel in half and draped it over the seat.

Sharky gave her the all-clear signal. “It’s time to roll, Fin. Have a seat, buddy.”

The cat’s ears flattened, and he shot Sharky an annoyed look.

“We’re not going anywhere until you’re sittin’ down.”

Fin hunched his back and flopped down in the basket.

“That’s more like it.” Sharky glanced over his shoulder. “You ready, Millster?”

“As ready as I’ll ever be.”

Sharky hit the gas and Millie's head snapped back. She could hear something pop near the back of her neck. "Sharky Kiveski! You promised this was going to be an easy ride."

"It is. Sheesh. I'm barely pressing the throttle. I can't help it if the Flamethrower has too much power."

"A snail's pace. You promised a snail's pace," she reminded him.

"You're such a party pooper." Sharky eased off the throttle, and they crept along, sticking close to the deck's outer edge.

Millie could feel her cheeks warm as passengers inside the *Waves Buffet* stopped and stared at Sharky and Fin on his black scooter with a bright red flame splashed across the side, towing Millie and the water-logged scooter.

Sharky reached the plexiglass panel dividers and veered to the right.

Anticipating the sudden shift, Millie tightened her grip and successfully steered past it.

"How you doing back there?" Sharky hollered.

"As good as can be expected." Millie made a sharp left, coasting past the second divider. She let out the breath she was holding. It was clear sailing for as far as she could see.

The "tow-er" and "tow-ee" got even more second glances as they cruised past the main pool deck.

Danielle was near the front, stomping and clomping through a lively set of dance moves while a group of passengers followed along. They shimmied to the left and did a fast twirl. Danielle stopped mid-twirl, her jaw dropping. "Millie?" echoed through the loudspeakers.

"Sharky?" Danielle stared. "I...sorry, everyone. It's not every day I see the ship's cruise director being towed by one of the maintenance supervisors."

Millie made a slicing motion across her neck. "It's not that exciting!" she hollered. "Carry on."

A man and woman in double scooters rolled up alongside them. They cut Sharky off, forcing him to slam on the brakes. He tooted the horn and waved them aside. "Watch where you're going! I have a disabled vehicle in tow."

The couple veered off to the side while the woman snatched her cell phone from her beach bag and snapped a picture of them.

Joy Turner, one of the ship's servers, strolled past. She came to an abrupt halt. "What in the world?"

"You don't want to know."

"Poor Millie." Joy grinned.

"The scooter is disabled."

"You're leaking." Joy pointed to the trail of water the scooter was leaving behind.

"Wonderful."

It seemed like forever before they reached the opposite end of the open deck.

"Can we pick it up? We're drawing attention."

"You're driving too fast. Can we pick it up?" Sharky mocked. "How about, can you make up your mind? Do you want me to go slow or fast?"

"A little faster."

Sharky picked up speed. The bank of elevators was in sight, but instead of heading toward them, he kept going.

"Aren't we taking the elevators?"

"Not those. They don't go all the way down."

"Crud. You're right." Millie's shoulders sagged as she resigned herself to the fact she and Sharky would soon be the talk of the ship.

Finally, they reached the forward bank of elevators. Sharky hopped off and untied the tow rope.

"What are you doing?"

"Both scooters won't fit in the elevator at the same time. I'm gonna get you in first and then meet you at the bottom." Sharky pushed from behind while Millie steered the scooter inside. "I'm not a fan..."

"Of elevators." Sharky finished her sentence. "I know, but we don't have much choice. You can do it, Millie."

"Fine." Millie waited for him to clear the elevator. She jabbed the deck zero button, and the doors closed.

The elevator stopped on deck ten and a group of passengers started to join her until discovering there wasn't enough room. "Sorry folks. This is a disabled scooter," she apologized.

"No problem." They backed away, and the door closed.

Please keep going, Millie whispered as the elevator continued its descent. It stopped again on deck seven. Two women started to squeeze in and paused, appearing uncertain.

"I think you can fit." Millie motioned them inside.

"Are you sure?"

"Yeah." She held the open button. "Where are you going?"

"Guest services," the woman said. "Where are you headed?"

"To maintenance."

"Oh." The woman's eyes grew round as saucers as she stared at the water puddling on the floor. "I heard someone drove a scooter into the pool. Is this it?"

"It is," Millie confirmed.

"Who would do such a thing?" the second woman asked.

"I don't know, but hopefully it's an isolated incident."

The doors opened, and the women wished Millie luck before exiting.

Thankfully, the elevator made it to the designated deck without further incident. She hopped off and pushed it out, waiting for Sharky.

Five minutes passed, and there was still no sign of him. She reached for her radio, planning to track him down when the doors opened and he and Fin emerged. "I thought you were joyriding in the elevator."

"I had to wait until I found an empty one."

"Where are you taking this?"

"To the laundry room," Sharky said. "They have some super sized fans. I was thinking I could dry it out first and then pop in a couple of extra batteries to see if it fires up."

Millie climbed back on as Sharky secured the tow rope. He and Fin took off. Unlike the upper deck obstacle course, there weren't any other near collisions, and they made good time.

Rahul, the laundry supervisor, met them near the door. "Millie, Sharky." He patted Fin's head. "How can I help you?"

Sharky jabbed his thumb at the waterlogged scooter. "This baby ended up in the bottom of the lido deck's rear pool. I was hoping I could borrow one of your fans to dry it out."

"Yes, of course." Rahul started to lead them toward the back and Millie stopped them. "I should probably get going."

"No problem. We can handle it from here." Sharky lifted a hand for a high-five. "Thanks, Millie."

"You're welcome." Millie slapped his hand. "Now, all we need to do is figure out who decided it would be fun to destroy someone else's property."

Chapter 7

It was all hands on deck as Millie and the entertainment staff began making the last-minute preparations for Santa's Turkey Trot Parade. Danielle arrived and jumped in, helping arrange the participants and displays in an orderly fashion.

There were mini floats and musicians, glitz and glamour, flash and fun. A buzz of excitement filled the air and someone broke out in an enthusiastic rendition of Majestic Cruise Line's official holiday song, Turkey Trot.

"You're smiling." Millie turned to find a pirate, rocking a silky ruffled shirt with red slacks and knee-high black boots, watching her. "Aye matey."

Millie pointed to Felix's black eyepatch. "I thought you were going for the jester look."

"Until I found this awesome gem in the back of the wardrobe closet." He brandished a sword and rubbed his finger over the plastic tip. "There'll be no more smilin' or I'll be taking ya' up to the promenade to walk the plank."

"This is a great costume." Millie playfully tugged on his black bandana.

"Because this is going to be fun, fun, fun," Felix sang in his falsetto pirate voice. "Who doesn't love a parade?"

"Me, but only when I'm in charge of it," Millie joked.

Danielle made her way over. "It's almost time to hit the parade route."

"Please, God," Millie prayed aloud. "Let things go smoothly."

"I have an idea." Danielle patted her radio. "Why don't you lead the parade route and I'll bring up the rear?"

“I have an even better idea,” Felix said. “The parade route runs through the center atrium.”

“It does,” Millie confirmed. “Passengers will have plenty of room to gather along the railings and have a bird’s-eye view from above.”

“What about the crow’s nest?”

Tucked away on the atrium’s upper deck was a small balcony barely visible and inaccessible to passengers.

“You’re right.” Danielle snapped her fingers. “We’ll be able to see it all from up there. I can hang out in the crow’s nest and monitor almost the entire parade.”

“I hadn’t even thought about that. I’ll be on deck five. You take deck seven with the overview. I’m sure between the two of us, we can handle anything that might come up.”

“Nothing will, my dears,” Felix assured them. “But it doesn’t hurt to be proactive.”

An even better idea—or as Andy would call it—a "brilliant," idea occurred to Millie. "Do you think you can record it with your cell phone? It might cheer Andy up if we sent him a recording of the parade."

Danielle grabbed her cell phone and tapped the screen. "I have plenty of battery left. I'll be able to get some great shots from that angle."

With a plan in place, Danielle hurried off to get into position.

The voices in the room grew louder, reaching an elevated pitch. Millie reached into her pocket, pulled out her whistle and gave it two short blasts.

"Listen up!" she yelled. "It's showtime. I'm counting on all of you to wow the passengers, get them excited about the parade and in the holiday spirit. When this is over, I want passengers stopping us everywhere, telling us how much they enjoyed the show."

Millie paused before continuing. "Is everyone ready?"

"Yeah!" the enthusiastic reply echoed back.

"I can't hear you." Millie playfully tilted her head and placed her hand to her ear. "I said...is everybody READY?"

"YES!!" A thunderous echo rang out and the entertainment staff clapped loudly.

Millie took a deep breath. "Let's move it on out. It's time to get this show on the road!"

*****

The carolers caroled, the drummers drummed, the turkeys trotted. Santa was comfortably seated in his high-back chair with Mrs. Claus by his side while a trio of elves and Rudolph pranced around them.

There were jesters and jugglers. Mermaids and mermen tossed wrapped pieces of candy to the children and Millie, who led it all, passed out candy canes to those within reach.

Wherever she looked, passengers were smiling. The junior passengers stood watching, their eyes shining brightly, and she knew then that Andy had masterfully crafted a memorable holiday parade.

At the halfway point, passengers who had been practicing for a flash mob fell into step with the choreographers. They twirled, stomped and sashayed, all flawlessly keeping step with the holiday tune.

The crowd quickly picked up the beat, clapping along.

Millie started to relax, certain the event would go off without a hitch now that they had reached the halfway point.

She passed out her last candy cane and jogged ahead to direct the parade participants toward the exits, seamlessly moving the cast and staff forward for the long trek down and back around to the starting point and staging area.

The holiday song segued into a catchy tune and she hummed along. Drummers to the left set of stairs. Jesters to the right.

Even more smiling faces appeared, and it warmed Millie's heart to know she had helped spread a little joy and cheer not only to the passengers but also to the hardworking Siren of the Seas' staff and crew.

Millie grabbed her radio. "Hey, Danielle."

"Go ahead, Millie."

"How is everything on your end?"

"Running like clockwork. I'm getting some great video. I can't wait to send it to Andy. Where are you?"

"Standing at the end of the parade route, directing everyone to the stairwells and exits so we don't get jammed up."

"Cool. I can see the tail end of the parade now. Santa and Mrs. Claus successfully circled back around and are on the last float."

Millie bounced on the tips of her toes, straining to catch a glimpse of the stars of the parade. She could make out the tippy top of Santa's bright red and white hat.

The crowd cheered and clapped. A rousing rendition of a classic Santa Claus song filled the atrium and spilled over into the hall where Millie stood watching.

"Hey, Millie. Are you still there?"

"I'm here, Danielle."

"Just to confirm what I vaguely remember, can you tell me what the woman who went missing looks like?"

"She's in her thirties, if I had to guess. Harper is tall with long blond hair. Why?"

"Because I think I saw her."

Millie's scalp tingled. "You saw her. Where?"

"In the parade. She's right in front of Santa's float, wearing some sort of crazy outfit."

"What color is it?" Millie craned her neck, struggling to pin down the exact spot Danielle was talking about. "What does her costume look like?"

"Like a homemade toga with Mardi Gras beads strung across it. She's exiting the atrium. You should be able to see her any second. You can't miss her outfit."

Millie slipped off to the side, her eyes darting back and forth as she searched for the toga-clad missing passenger.

A wisp of platinum blond hair appeared and then the willowy blonde emerged. A soft smile framed her face, yet her eyes were half-closed, as if she was in some sort of trance, which was probably a good thing since she hadn't yet spotted Millie.

Closer. The woman drew closer. As if sensing she was being watched, her eyes flew open.

Their eyes met.

Harper smirked as she thumbed her nose at Millie. In the blink of an eye, the woman did an about-face and made a mad dash in the other direction, pushing her way past the reindeer and marching band.

"Wait!" Millie struggled to keep a visual on the woman as she wound her way past the passengers and participants. "Excuse me. Pardon me."

The crowd closed in on Millie and her heart plummeted as she watched Harper pick up speed, moving against the flow of foot traffic.

"Millie, where are you?"

"I'm trapped in the crowd. She's getting away."

"I'll see if I can tail her." Danielle's voice grew ragged. "She exited the atrium and is making a run for the main corridor."

"Heading forward or aft?"

"Forward. Forward on deck five."

"I'm still moving but it's a slow go." Millie continued pushing through but it was a losing battle. Not only was she surrounded by the ship's crew, but passengers were following behind, chatting with the entertainers.

Millie ducked down and scrunched in, squeezing through a narrow gap. Finally, she reached the center atrium, her eyes darting to the empty crow's nest and then back toward the spot where she'd last glimpsed the missing woman.

She skirted the edge of the crowd, her eyes scanning both sides of the corridor as she raced toward the front of the ship. "I'm in the corridor. Where are you, Danielle?"

"At the end." Danielle stepped into view and began waving her arms.

Millie ran toward her. "Well?"

"She got away." Danielle held up a white sheet. "She left this behind."

Millie blinked rapidly. “She’s running around naked?”

“No. She was wearing a cream-colored jogging suit beneath it.”

The women circled the atrium, each heading in opposite directions and met up at their starting point.

“She’s gone,” Millie said.

“The good news is we’ve confirmed she’s on board the ship. Judging by the way she took off, she seems to be in good health.”

“Where exactly did you find the toga sheet?”

Danielle led her to the hall. “Right about here.”

Millie stepped over to a cozy seating area in front of a large ocean view window.

Crunch. She jerked her foot back and discovered she’d stepped on something. She bent down to pick it up. “Look what I found?” Millie held up a set of scooter keys.

Chapter 8

"This confirms what we already suspected." Millie jangled the keys. "Ten bucks says these belong to the scooter found at the bottom of the pool."

"I'll run downstairs to take care of the parade stuff if you want to track down the scooter to see if it's a match," Danielle said.

"Thanks. It shouldn't take long. I'll catch up with you. Putting the props and costumes away is going to take time." Millie turned to go and paused. "I thought of something. You said you recorded the parade?"

Danielle patted her pocket. "It's all on my cell phone. I'll send a copy to Andy when we reach Aruba and I have better cell reception."

"Can you send me a copy? I want to see if I can spot Rothshield."

"Consider it done, but again, it will have to wait until we reach port."

The women parted ways, and Millie made a mad dash for the laundry center to track Rahul down.

"The scooter is still drying out." The head of the laundry center escorted her to the drying room. It was like walking into a sauna, threatening to cause Millie's claustrophobia to kick in.

Rahul, noting Millie's obvious discomfort, led her out of the area. "Sharky is coming back in a couple hours to check on it, although we noticed the keys are missing, which could present a problem."

"Not anymore." Millie pulled the keys from her pocket. "I think we found them. I'm also hot on the trail of the person responsible for the reckless joyride."

"That is wonderful," Rahul said. "Let's see if your hunch is correct."

As suspected, the keys fit perfectly. Millie flipped the switch. Nothing happened. "Crud. Hopefully, Sharky can get the scooter up and running and return it to the passenger."

"It will not work now, Miss Millie. Sharky removed the batteries."

"Duh. I should've remembered that." Millie handed Rahul the keys. "Can you please do me a favor and give these to Sharky?"

"I most certainly will."

Millie thanked him and ran backstage, where she was greeted by what could only be described as organized chaos. Danielle was in the thick of it, struggling to inventory the costumes and make sure the parade's props were returned to their proper location.

"How's the stash and dash going?" Millie asked as she came up beside her.

"Stash and dash?"

"Stash the stuff and dash out for the next activity."

"It looks chaotic, but it's actually running smoothly." Danielle waited for the next staff member to return their costume and head out. "Was the scooter key a fit?"

"Yes. We now know two things. Harper Rothshield is alive and well, and causing problems."

"It seems to me the woman is unstable. Has Patterson chatted with the group she boarded with?"

"Her friends and boyfriend," Millie said. "He has. Maybe it's time for me to stick my nose in. What did you do with Harper's discarded toga outfit?"

"It's on the makeup counter in the back."

"We'll hang onto it until I can catch up with Patterson and turn it over to him."

The crowd dwindled, and finally, Danielle and Millie were alone.

"Patterson mentioned Harper and her friends attended the singles get-together the first day. Are we still accepting online signups?"

"Yeah, but it's strictly voluntary. It gives me a general idea of the headcount. Do you want to see what I have?"

"If you don't mind."

Danielle tapped the top of her activity app and twisted her wrist so Millie could see. "This is today's list."

Millie scrolled through the screen, noting none of those listed were Harper or her friends. "Neither of Harper's friends are on the list."

"Like I said, it's voluntary. Passengers aren't required to sign up, although I think the singles like it, especially if they're hoping someone they're interested in is attending."

"I wouldn't mind hosting on the off-chance one of them will be there." Millie consulted her schedule. "I have a VIP ship tour coming up."

"Sweet. You host the mingle and I'll handle your tour."

"Have you done the toilet paper icebreaker game yet?"

"Nope. It's all yours."

Millie finished the costume and prop inventory checklist and ran upstairs, making a quick pit stop at one of the public restrooms to grab some rolls of toilet paper before continuing to the Marseille Lounge for the mix and mingle.

A small group was already waiting, and Millie greeted them as she strolled toward the stage. More arrived and by the time she started, the place was packed.

“Hello, everyone. I’m Millie, your cruise director. Please help yourself to the tea, lemonade and light snacks over by the bar.”

Taking a rough head count, she gave the group a few minutes to socialize and then split them up into groups. Making her way from one to the next, she explained how the toilet paper game worked, got the ball rolling, and moved on.

By design, there was an equal split of men and women in each group. Following the game, she switched it up, separating the attendees by geographic location—passengers outside the United States, and then all four corners...north, south, east and west.

After the groups were assembled, she asked them to form a circle. Each person shared an interesting piece of information about where they were from, while the others in the group had to guess the name of the city or town.

Millie headed to the bar to grab a glass of water. A woman who was part of the southern group caught up with her. "Millie?"

"Yes."

"I'm Sierra Geldman."

"Hello, Sierra."

"I'm Harper Rothshield's friend."

"Harper Rothshield." Millie chose her words carefully. "Harper, the passenger who is somewhere on board the ship and doesn't want to be located?"

"Yeah. She–uh–she wasn't a big fan of yours."

"I'm sorry to hear that. We chatted before she decided to go into hiding. She claims there was a misunderstanding about an incident at the nightclub the first night you boarded and while we were discussing what happened, she accused me of calling her a liar."

"Harper is sensitive to criticism," Sierra said. "Anyway, she's been sending me texts and pictures."

"Texts and pictures of what?"

Sierra shrugged. "Random stuff. The midnight chocolate buffet, the night sky."

"Do you know where she's hiding?"

"No." Sierra shook her head. "I wish I did."

"What about Bryce, one of the other people you're traveling with. Does he know where she is?"

"I don't think so. She's mad at him, so she's not answering his calls or texts. At least that's what he said. I planned to call Mr. Patterson, the head of security, but thought I would mention it to you since Harper keeps bringing your name up."

Millie's heart skipped a beat. "My name?"

"She found out you're the captain's wife and seems to think you're targeting her."

"I'm targeting her? For what possible reason?"

The woman wrinkled her nose. “She can be a little paranoid. Once she becomes fixated on someone, it usually means trouble. It doesn’t help that she’s off her meds and mad at Bryce.”

“Why would she go off her medication?” Millie asked.

“She got ticked at the doctors at the rehab and skipped out, which is how we ended up booking this cruise. She said she needed a break. Once she starts on one of her downward spirals, it’s hard to get her back on track. And…” Sierra’s voice faded.

“And what?’ Millie prompted.

“She’s in between gigs.”

“In between gigs?”

“Television stardom. Harper was on a reality show and thought she was a shoo-in for some other gigs. They fell through and she’s freaking out.” The woman lowered her voice. “When they find out about her past substance abuse, they don’t want anything to do with her.”

Millie completely understood their concern.

"Harper's not a bad person. She just has problems..."

"With anyone she doesn't agree with and is unable to take responsibility for her actions, not to mention the substance abuse issue."

"Yeah. I know this isn't your problem, but I thought I should warn you," Sierra said. "Mr. Patterson said they're trying to track her down, but it won't be easy if Harper doesn't want to be found."

Millie thanked her and watched her return to the group, mulling over all that Sierra had said. For some reason, the disturbed woman was fixated on Millie—as the captain's wife.

If her plan was to remain in hiding and continue causing trouble, what would she do next?

As soon as the party ended, Millie tracked Patterson down and caught up with him in Andy's office.

"Harper Rothshield is alive and well." Millie handed him the discarded toga. "She was in the parade."

"In the parade?" Patterson frowned.

"Wearing this. She took Danielle and me on a wild goose chase and left this, along with the keys to the waterlogged scooter, behind for us to find."

"Are you sure it was her?"

"One hundred percent. Sierra Geldman, one of Harper's friends, chatted with me at the singles get-together. For some reason, Harper has it in for me. She found out I'm the captain's wife and it set her off."

"I've been in contact with Ms. Rothshield's family. She's also sent them random texts, threatening to embarrass them and make headline news. Based on her background, it could be a publicity stunt," Patterson said. "All available security staff members are on high alert. We'll continue searching every nook and cranny of the ship. How she's staying one step ahead of us is beyond me."

"Lots of practice. From what her friend said, this isn't the first time Harper has done some strange things." Millie tapped her chin. "Looking back, Sierra made an interesting comment. I think it may be a clue."

Chapter 9

"What sort of clue?" Patterson asked.

"I questioned Sierra about Bryce, and if he knew where she might be hiding. She said she didn't think so," Millie said. "Don't you think that's an odd answer?"

Patterson thought about it. "Maybe. Maybe not."

"I mean, he either knows where she is or he doesn't."

"I've already chatted with him. He swears he doesn't." Patterson consulted his watch. "I'm late for a meeting. Is there anything else?"

"That's it for now." After Patterson left, Millie logged into Andy's scheduler and accessed his work calendar. She clicked on the upcoming events and then worked her way through the list. Although signing up wasn't a requirement for some or even half the scheduled activities, there were others which required passengers to pre-register—namely pay-to-participate events. The Chef's Table, a gourmet dinner with a designated chef, Culinary Creations by Annette, the casino's slot tournaments.

She located Bryce Bridges' account and pulled up his list of onboard charges, taking note of the items he'd purchased...souvenirs from the gift shop, cash from the casino, specialty coffee from the coffee shop.

One in particular caught her eye. It was in the pending transaction screen. Millie double-clicked on the link. It was a pre-registration for the evening's champagne art auction. She switched screens and pulled up her schedule.

Although it wasn't her event, she also wasn't scheduled to host anything during that time slot. Millie clicked on his account folio and studied his photograph. He was a nice-looking guy with a warm smile and crinkly eyes, as if he smiled a lot.

She exited the screens and grabbed her lanyard. It was time to chat with Harper's boyfriend.

*****

Millie arrived at the High Seas Art Gallery before the gallery's host and greeted her as she unlocked the door.

"I'm sorry to hear about Andy's emergency leave. How is it going?"

Millie patted her head. "I still have all my hair. Check back with me at the end of the voyage. It might be a different story."

"I heard the parade was fabulous. I'm sorry I missed it."

"It was fantastic, if I do say so myself." Millie followed the woman inside. "I have some time in between events and wondered if you needed help."

"I can always use an extra hand."

"Perfect. I'll collect the invitations if you want to make sure the beverages and auction prints are ready to go." Millie returned to the entrance and began greeting the guests. "Welcome to High Seas Art Gallery. Feel free to browse the available artwork."

It was an equal split of passengers, mainly couples, while there were a few solo attendees thrown into the mix. The start of the auction drew near and Bryce Bridges still hadn't checked in.

Millie started to slip inside when she noticed a man strolling down the corridor, moving at a fast clip. It was Bryce.

She offered him a warm smile as he drew close. "You made it just in time."

"I was...unexpectedly detained by an important phone call." Bryce craned his neck. "Has the auction already started? I was hoping to preview a few of the pieces."

"Unfortunately, there won't be time, but I'm sure there will still be plenty to check out after it ends." Millie trailed behind, following Bryce into the crowded room. She stood off to the side while he slid into an empty seat midway between the front and back.

The auctioneer moved at a rapid rate, belting out the bids and selling several pieces for top dollar. She studied the crowd, wondering if some of the bidders were plants, put in place to bid up the prices in the hopes a passenger would get into a bidding war for their favorite piece.

The ship's art gallery was run by a third party company and she'd heard rumblings of questionable tactics being used to move the prints. Regardless, art and value were in the eye of the beholder. Who could say what a piece was worth? To Millie, it wasn't any different from antiques or collectibles. The art was worth whatever a buyer was willing to pay for it.

Near the end of the auction, Millie answered a frantic call, ironing out a minor issue between the jazz music ensemble and the country music duo on board, both of whom believed they were supposed to set up in the center atrium.

The champagne art auction wrapped up and several guests, including Bryce, lingered.

Millie wandered over. "Have you found a piece you can't live without?"

He shot a glance over his shoulder. "More than one, actually. My girlfriend loves Varney Boutell. Her birthday is coming up, and I was hoping to surprise her by purchasing one of his original works."

Millie's scalp tingled. "I've never heard of Varney Boutell. What sort of artist is he? Abstract? Realism? Pop Art?"

"He does a mishmash. I wouldn't call it one style in particular. I don't like making impulse purchases and would have preferred to preview the art ahead of time."

"I don't blame you," Millie replied. "That's very thoughtful of you to want to find a special gift for your girlfriend."

After he left, Millie mulled over their conversation. Obviously, he was still of the opinion they were a couple if he was considering purchasing a birthday present for her. He appeared surprisingly calm and collected for someone whose girlfriend was in hiding and showing signs of instability.

Millie thought about what Harper's friend, Sierra, had told her. The woman wanted to be seen, to be noticed yet not necessarily found, but for what purpose? To jumpstart her failing career?

Perhaps the scooter incident was the tip of the iceberg and the woman planned to ramp up her antics. The key was to figure out her next move and catch her in the act.

A chilling thought occurred to Millie. One of the scariest scenarios on board a ship was fire. Another was the bridge being hijacked. She remembered an incident years ago when one of the ship's employees plotted with a group to overthrow the Siren of the Seas.

Fortunately, they were caught before they could follow through with their plan. It had been a frightening incident, particularly after discovering someone on the inside was working alongside them to gain access to the bridge and ship's captains.

Of course, Harper Rothshield didn't have access to the bridge unless...

Millie grabbed her cell phone and dialed Danielle's number. "Hey, Danielle. How did the ship tour go?"

"Great. Several passengers asked about you."

"Did you tour the bridge?"

"Yeah. It was our last stop."

“Was anyone dressed in a toga or wearing a hoodie part of the group?”

“As in, anyone suspicious like our MIA passenger Harper?”

“Correct.”

“Nope. All were past guests. None were young, tall and blond.”

“Great.” Millie pressed a hand to her chest. “My gut tells me Harper isn’t done causing trouble on board the ship.”

“Seriously? So the scooter sinking was only the beginning?”

Millie told Danielle about her conversation with Sierra. “It appears she’s focused on me. I wouldn’t put it past her to try sneaking onto the bridge.”

“How many more tours do you have scheduled for this voyage?”

“Good question.” Millie tapped her scheduler app. “One more and I’m the tour guide.”

"I'm still keeping an eye out for her."

"We'll catch her. It's only a matter of time."

Later that evening, Millie slipped inside the dimly lit galley. Dinner had ended hours earlier, and the cavernous kitchen was eerily quiet. She heard a rustling noise coming from the dry storage room, which also served as Annette's office, and found her friend standing inside, clipboard in hand.

"Knock. Knock."

Annette spun around. "Hey, Millie. How was your day?"

"Long."

"Have a seat." Her friend patted the nearby barstool.

A sigh escaped Millie's lips. "My feet are killing me."

"I bet." Annette counted the cans of tomatoes and scribbled something on her clipboard. "I heard the parade was a smashing success."

"It was. I'm not sure who enjoyed it more—the passengers or the crew."

"Have you found your MIA pain in the patootie passenger yet?"

"Pain in the patootie has-been reality television star. She's around." Millie filled her in, starting with her taking part in the parade and ending with Patterson's update.

"She's going to make headline news and it will involve the ship?" Annette shook her head. "At the very least, the woman is mentally unstable."

"As luck would have it, I'm on her radar."

"Because you called her out, and she didn't like it. She sounds like trouble with a capital 'T' plus some."

"And Siren of the Seas is getting caught in the crossfire." Millie blew air through thinned lips. "It's like knowing something bad is going to happen, but not knowing when or what."

"The scooter incident happened at night," Annette said.

"Early morning, when Harper knew few people would be around to catch her. It stands to reason she'll make her next move late at night or early in the morning. Unfortunately, we can't be everywhere all the time. She obviously has some experience in making herself scarce," Millie said. "She's only going to be seen when she wants to be."

"Are you hungry?" Annette set her clipboard aside. "I was going to grab a snack."

"Now that you mention it, I haven't eaten in a while."

Annette opened the refrigerator and began rummaging around. "How does cold quiche and fresh juice sound?"

"Like the perfect dinner." Millie slid off the stool and limped across the room. "I don't know how Andy's kept this crazy pace for all these years."

"How is Andy? Any word on a diagnosis?"

"Not yet. The doctors are still running tests." Millie helped Annette carry the platters to the counter. "I've been praying for him."

"Me too. He's a good guy. Cat and he have their whole lives ahead of them."

Millie eyed the plated pound cake near Amit's workstation. "What's that?"

"Amit's lemon pound cake. It's delish. Would you like to try a slice?"

"Sure. I love lemon cake."

Annette sliced two generous pieces and placed them on small salad plates. "He's almost perfected his recipe."

Millie studied the thick slice. She broke off a corner, savoring the tart lemon mingled with the sweet, crunchy glaze. "It's delicious. It has just the right amount of tartness. I love the crunchy topping."

"Thanks. We're adding the cake to our afternoon tea."

Ting. Millie's timer chimed while she was polishing off her quiche. "I'm running down to Andy's office to lock up and then head home."

"Good luck finding your troublemaker," Annette said. "There are only so many places she can hide. She'll eventually get caught."

"Hopefully sooner rather than later." Millie thanked her friend for lending an ear and sharing the food, and made the trek to the lower deck.

Slam. The outer theater door slammed, and Millie stumbled back, clutching her chest. It wasn't uncommon for employees who worked the late night shifts to stop by Andy's office or the dressing room to grab something they forgot on their way home.

Millie jumped again, this time at the sound of her cell phone chiming. She pulled it from her pocket and glanced at the screen. It was a text from Felix. *Where are you?*

Standing outside the theater, Millie texted back.

Wait for me. I'm on my way.

Millie hung out, waiting for Felix. She heard another sound, this one more of a clunking, as if a loose pipe was rattling. She shivered involuntarily and then silently scolded herself for being paranoid.

She was exhausted from a busy day on the run, handling the parade, worrying about Harper Rothshield, worrying about Andy.

From all appearances, Rothshield had it made. A promising career, fame, a good-looking, not to mention thoughtful, boyfriend.

To Millie, it was proof money didn't make you happy. The woman had everything she could possibly want or need, yet it was clear she was unhappy. What sort of mental condition did she suffer from that required prescription medication?

While she waited, Millie did a quick search for specific symptoms Harper was exhibiting.

The woman was obviously delusional, believing Millie was picking on her. She skimmed through the other symptoms and began to suspect she was suffering from schizophrenia. "Poor thing," Millie whispered. "She needs help."

Quick steps echoed from the corridor, and Felix appeared. "Thanks for waiting for me. I think I left my keycard and ID card in the pirate costume's jacket pocket. Do you have the keys to the wardrobe closet?"

"I do. You caught me just in time. I was getting ready to lock up and head home."

Felix linked arms with Millie as they made their way toward the theater's double doors. "Everyone is raving about the parade. It was a huge hit."

"It turned out better than I thought it would. Danielle got it all on video. We're going to send a copy to Andy since he's the mastermind behind it all."

"And you helped execute it to perfection." Felix pressed his fingers to his lips. "If Andy ever decides to retire, you should apply for his job."

"Those are some awfully big shoes to fill."

"And you've proved you're the perfect person to fill them. Not that I don't absolutely adore our commander-in-chief, but I think you would be 'excel-ante' at it."

"Thanks, Felix. Your friendship and support mean a lot to me." Millie eased the doors open and stepped inside the dark theater.

Squeak. Something squished beneath her feet. Felix must've noticed the same. "Does the floor seem wet to you?" he whispered.

"It does." Millie took another tentative step, creating another squeak. "Where's the light switch?" She felt along the side of the wall and flipped the switch.

Bright lights illuminated the empty theater and Millie looked down, a sinking sensation settling in the pit of her stomach. She said the first thing that popped into her head. "Harper Rothshield."

Chapter 10

Millie's shoe squished again as a fine mist coated her face.

Felix warily lifted his gaze toward the ceiling, easily identifying where the water was coming from. "The emergency sprinkler system has been tripped."

Millie snatched her radio from her belt. "Maintenance department. Is anyone in maintenance available?"

"Go ahead, Millie. Reef here. What's up?"

"Hey, Reef. I'm standing in the main theater. The sprinkler system is on. The floor is wet and Felix and I are getting misted."

"Is it coming from the ceiling?"

"Yes," Millie and Felix answered in unison.

"There's a fine mist coming from the ceiling," Millie confirmed.

"I'm on my way. I'll meet you there."

Felix ran a light hand across the back of a seat. "The seats are still dry, which means the sprinklers just came on."

"I heard a door slam right before you radioed me. Someone was in here messing around." Millie backtracked to the nearby women's restroom.

The automatic lights triggered as soon as she stepped inside, illuminating the interior. Millie ran to the stall at the end and flung the door open, half expecting Harper to pop out and attack her.

She worked her way all the way to the end, only to find the stalls were all empty.

Felix appeared in the doorway. "What are you doing?"

"I think the passenger who's been causing trouble set off the sprinkler system. Would you mind checking the men's restroom?"

"Not at all." Felix took off in the opposite direction while Millie searched the theater's outer corridor. If Harper had messed with the sprinklers, she was long gone. And if Millie hadn't gone back to make sure Andy's office and the theater were locked, would the sprinklers have stayed on all night?

Reef, accompanied by a small army of maintenance men, arrived within minutes. "How bad is it?"

"I don't know yet. You'll need to shut the water off."

"There's an emergency valve in the back."

Millie followed Reef and the men into the theater and over to a panel on the far wall, near the sound equipment.

"Someone pried the cover off and triggered the sensor." Reef tapped the top of the damaged cover.

"What would it take to get the cover off?" Millie asked.

"A flathead screwdriver or the claw end of a hammer."

"What about a metal fingernail file?"

"That might work too. Why would someone want to turn the sprinklers on?"

"To destroy the ship's property." Millie clenched her jaw and stared at the damaged cover. "If I hadn't come back here to make sure everything was locked up, this could have stayed on all night. Isn't there some sort of alarm system that triggers when the sprinklers are activated?"

"Only for the main ones," Reef said. "This is an auxiliary system and not capable of switching on unless the main ones are turned on."

"In other words, it's a backup system."

"Correct," Reef confirmed.

"So someone would have to know that or take a really lucky guess," Millie said.

"Yep. I'm going with the luck angle. Whoever it was, wasn't all that smart to smash the box." Reef explained that had they touched any sort of metal to the switch on the other side, they would have been zapped.

"By an electrical shock?"

"Yeah. It probably wouldn't have been powerful enough to kill them, but they would've gotten a pretty good zap, enough to knock them flat on their back."

With the sprinkler system off, Reef and his men began assessing the damage.

Meanwhile, Millie and Felix continued making their way backstage. She held her breath, bracing for the worst, as she stepped inside Andy's office. Fortunately, it appeared nothing had been tampered with.

"Let's see if we can find your keys." Millie unlocked the storage closet. "The pirate costumes are on the left."

Felix began rummaging around inside. "Here it is." He held up the lanyard. "Thanks, Millie. You're the best."

"You're welcome. I'm going to check Andy's office one last time and call it a day."

"I'll go with you, just in case."

Touched by Felix's concern for her safety, Millie patted his arm. "Have I ever told you what a good friend you are?"

"We're besties," Felix said. "Besties always watch each other's backs." He motioned toward the theater's seating area. "Do you think the troubled chickadee is behind this?"

"I'm almost certain of it. I think she's disturbed and determined to cause trouble. The sooner Patterson and his men track her down, the better." Millie left Felix near the elevators and trudged up the stairs to the bridge, all the while mulling over the most recent incident.

Someone had sneaked into the theater and triggered the sprinkler system. If Harper was behind it, she was falling into a pattern of doing her dirty work after hours, when most of the ship's passengers and crew were asleep.

Back home, Millie filled Nic in on the damage and shared her thoughts about who was behind it.

"Patterson and his men are doing their best to find her but haven't had any luck so far."

Millie stepped onto the balcony, and Nic followed her out. "The scooter incident was annoying but easily resolved. If the sprinkler system had gone undetected until morning, there would be much more damage."

"The water would eventually run down to the stage and ruin equipment, not to mention the stage itself," Nic said. "It appears we're going to have to add extra security staff to the night shift."

A small detail nagged in the back of Millie's mind. There was some clue trying to surface but her tired brain was too drained to muddle through it. "Tomorrow is a new day. Hopefully, Ms. Rothshield isn't roaming around plotting her next act of destruction."

Millie tossed and turned that night, wondering what Rothshield would do next. She was certain she'd almost crossed paths with the woman outside the theater. If she had only gone down there a few minutes earlier, she could have caught her in the act. Patterson could have locked her up or made sure she remained inside her cabin for the duration of the cruise.

But she was still out there. The fact Millie was on the woman's radar was concerning. What would she do next? That was the big question.

Perhaps another chat with Harper's friends was in order. Maybe they could shed some light on what was going through the woman's mind and provide Millie with a clue about what she might try next.

Chapter 11

Because it was a port day, Nic was required to be on the bridge to meet with the harbor pilot early the next morning.

Millie wasn't far behind, certain that the ship's passengers were eager to go ashore, having a full day—early morning until late evening—to enjoy Oranjestad and all that Aruba had to offer. There was snorkeling and diving, coves and caves, not to mention mountains to explore via dune buggy.

Because it was a docking port, access to the gangway was open to everyone, not just the excursion groups, and there was already a long line snaking up the stairs when she arrived to see passengers off.

Several stopped to ask questions about shipboard time, back on board, and even a few who asked for her personal recommendation to make the most of their island visit. Beyond the gangway, Millie could see several tour guides holding numbered signs and directing people to the buses.

"Hello, Millie."

Millie whirled around and found Sierra Geldman standing to her right. "Hello, Sierra. You're heading out for the day?"

Sierra patted her beach bag. "I'm ready to have some fun in the sun."

"It's going to be a beautiful day." Millie extended her hand to the woman standing next to her. "Hello. I don't believe we've met yet."

The woman greeted her with a smile. "Millie. I've been meaning to tell you we've enjoyed all the activities so far. I'm Kimberly Frye."

"It's nice to meet you, Kimberly." Millie glanced around. "There's still no sign of Harper, your traveling companion?"

"No. She's keeping a low profile," Kimberly replied. "Bryce thinks she sneaked into their cabin sometime last night."

"Oh?" Millie perked up. "Why does he think that?"

"Because more of her stuff went missing."

Millie played dumb. "Refresh my memory. Bryce is..."

"He's Harper's boyfriend and my brother," Kimberly said. "The ship's head of security thinks he has something to do with Harper's disappearance, but he doesn't understand. She's disappeared before. She'll surface when she's ready."

"Where is Bryce now?"

"He's meeting us off the ship after stopping by the security department's office to let them know about Harper going into the cabin."

"Does he know around what time that may have been?"

The women exchanged a glance. "It was late, after the nightclub closed."

Millie made a mental note to check the keycard, although she was certain Patterson was already monitoring it for activity.

"Are you hosting the mix and mingle later?" Sierra asked.

"I'm not sure. Will you be there?"

"Yeah. We've made some new friends. In fact, we're meeting up with them for the beach excursion. Harper is missing out."

"Have fun and don't forget the sunscreen."

Finally, the crowds thinned, and Millie headed upstairs. She swung by the guest services desk and waited until Nikki was free.

"Hey, Millie. I was lucky enough to be working when the parade went through yesterday. It was awesome."

"I'm glad you enjoyed it. You had one of the best views," Millie said.

"I did. So what's up?"

"I was wondering if you could look up a passenger's cabin number for me."

"Sure. Who is it?"

"Harper Rothshield."

Nikki's eyes flitted to Millie's face. "The missing woman."

"Yeah. Her boyfriend mentioned she may have stopped by their cabin at some point last night. I was thinking I could swing by there and check it out."

"Sure." Nikki reached for the mouse. She grabbed a slip of paper and began jotting something down. "Here's the cabin number."

Millie thanked her, stepped off to the side, and pulled up her schedule. Unfortunately, she was booked solid until lunchtime. Taking a look around would have to wait.

*****

Near noon, Millie was finally able to carve out some free time. Her first step was to find out if the coast was clear and called down to the gangway.

"Gabe at the gangway. How can I assist you?"

"Hi Gabe. This is Millie Armati. I was wondering if you could check to see if three passengers are still off the ship." Millie gave him Sierra, Kimberly and Bryce's names.

"They still haven't returned, Mrs. Armati."

"That's all I needed to know." Millie thanked him and called Danielle next. "Where are you?"

"In the middle of a bingo session. What's up?"

"I'm in front of the piano bar contemplating heading down to Harper's cabin to search it. I need help."

"To search it? I'm sure Patterson's already done that."

"He has, but I found out Harper surfaced long enough to grab some more stuff from her cabin. At least that's what the women who are traveling with her told me."

"Why not tell Patterson and let him check it out?" Danielle asked.

"He left the ship to attend some sort of meeting. I'm not sure when he's coming back. Bryce, the boyfriend is off the ship, which means now is the optimal opportunity to sneak in."

"I'm not free for another fifteen minutes."

Millie consulted her watch. "The clock is ticking. I want to get in and out."

A familiar figure strolled past, and Millie started trailing behind. "Don't worry about it. I think I have someone who can help."

"Good luck. You know how these search-the-cabin-and-get-busted scenarios go down."

"Yeah, but I think I'm in good shape. I've confirmed all three of Harper's traveling companions are currently off the ship." Millie ended the call. She ran after Joy Turner and caught up with her near the stairwell.

"Hey, Millie. I haven't seen you around much. I heard Andy's on medical leave and that you were filling in."

"He is, and I've been going nonstop."

"I hope he's going to be all right."

"Me too." Millie lowered her voice. "I have a quick favor to ask. I need a lookout."

"A lookout?"

"I want to take a quick peek inside a passenger's cabin." Millie motioned to the cart Joy was pushing. "You're handling room service deliveries?"

"I am. I just finished up and was on my way back to the galley."

Millie eyed the cart and its contents. "This might work out perfectly. If you can spare about ten minutes, I want to run down to deck five."

"Which is where I just came from."

"Even better. You have a valid reason for being there." Millie nudged Joy toward the corridor. "You take the service elevator and I'll meet you on deck five."

"There's room for both of us."

"I'm not a fan of elevators. In fact, I do my best to avoid them whenever possible."

"Oh. Gotcha."

They reached the crew corridor. Millie jabbed the down button and waited for Joy and her cart to squeeze inside. "See you in a sec."

She bolted down the steps, easily beating the slow service elevators. The doors opened and Joy emerged. "Which cabin are you sneaking into?"

Millie consulted Nikki's note. "Cabin 5114."

"We'll need to go this way." Joy pushed the cart along, with Millie hustling to keep up. The empty dishes rattled loudly, creating so much noise a couple up ahead turned around to see where it was coming from.

"We're drawing too much attention," Millie whispered.

"You're right." Joy grabbed the silverware and dropped them on top of the dinner napkin. The rattling stopped.

"Much better."

The women picked up the pace, moving at a fast clip toward the other end of the long hall.

Millie abruptly stopped. “This is it.”

“I’ll hang out here, pretending like I’m making a delivery,” Joy said.

“That’ll work.” Millie lifted her gaze to the surveillance cameras mounted above the corridor exit. “We’re being recorded, so you’ll want to make it appear as casual as possible.”

Joy started to look around, and Millie stopped her. “Don’t look. If you look, you’ll draw attention to us.”

“I take it you’ve done this a time or two,” Joy said.

“Or a half-dozen.” Millie gave Harper and Bryce’s cabin door a solid rap and waited. When no one answered, she slipped her master keycard into the slot and eased it open. “Keep your cell phone handy in case we need to communicate.”

"Good idea." Joy nervously patted her pocket. "I've never sneaked into a passenger's cabin before."

"You're not. I am."

"True. Good point. Good luck."

"Thanks. I won't be long." Millie slipped inside. She eased the door shut and ran her hand along the wall. She flipped the switch and bright lights illuminated the interior.

The cabin was tidy. In fact, it looked as if no one had ever slept there, which wasn't unusual if the room steward had already come through.

Millie started in the closets, rifling through the men's outfits—t-shirts, dress slacks, button-down shirts. She unzipped the large suitcase and peered inside. "Empty."

Moving on, she checked the desk drawers and sifted through the shelves' contents. Using her cell phone's flashlight, she shined it under the bed and confirmed the only thing beneath it were the lifejackets.

Millie stepped into the bathroom and opened the medicine cabinet. Inside were women's hair clips, a tube of sunscreen, dental floss, and a bottle of aftershave. There was one toothbrush and a travel-size tube of toothpaste.

She peeked inside the lower cabinets, noting an empty jewelry box and can of hairspray.

Millie eased the door open and started to step out when something caught her eye. She ran her hand along the inside of the shower door. It was still wet. Two towels hung on the bar next to it. She patted the fronts, discovering someone had recently used both of them.

A woman's shaver rested on the shower shelf. Millie picked it up, taking note of the fact the shaver was still wet.

Crash. A loud crash echoed from the hallway and Millie could hear voices. One of them belonged to Joy.

The cabin's doorknob rattled, and she froze in her tracks.

Chapter 12

The corridor grew quiet, and Millie seized the opportunity to make a mad dash for the balcony. She unlocked the slider door and tiptoed outside, leaving the heavy drapes drawn and praying whoever Joy had crossed paths with wasn't on their way in.

As luck would have it, Harper and Bryce's balcony cabin was dockside, and Millie could see passengers meandering along the side of the ship making their way to shore. She stood ramrod straight with her back against the balcony slider, hoping no one, including Dave Patterson, who was still ashore, would spot her.

She cautiously eased her cell phone from her pocket and tapped the screen. There was no text from Joy. Counting the long seconds, Millie gritted her teeth. Finally, she texted her lookout. *Is the coast clear?* She hit the send button and waited.

Ting. Joy was quick to reply. *Next door cabin neighbors have returned. Abort mission ASAP.*

On my way. Millie hit send and began inching her way toward the balcony door. Beads of sweat formed on her brow as she grasped the handle. She was almost home free.

The adjacent balcony door slid open, and Millie's heart skipped a beat.

"...and Bryce is almost certain Harper was in their cabin last night. This whole hiding out and destroying stuff has gotten out of hand." Millie recognized Sierra's voice and then Kimberly's reply. "Harper never should have skipped out of rehab. She only had a few more weeks and then she would've been home free."

"You know how much she hated that place," Sierra said. "What if she really went off her meds?"

"Bryce said her meds are gone, which means she must have them with her. Maybe she hooked up with some guy she met to get back at him. I know my brother, and it's going to backfire big time," Kimberly predicted.

"What do you think about the scooter they found at the bottom of the pool? Do you think Harper was the one who put it there?"

"No. I mean, she can seem whacko at times, but that would be a little extreme, even for Harper," Kimberly said.

Except for the fact we saw her in the parade, chased after her and found the scooter's keys next to her discarded toga, Millie silently replied.

"Either way, I think she's making a big mistake. Maybe she'll go back to waiting tables."

Kimberly laughed. "And how long did that job last?"

"Until Harper got tired of it. Where is Bryce?"

"He should be back any time now. He wanted to pick up some stuff at the gift shop near the dock. I told him we would meet him at the grill to grab a bite to eat."

Sierra approached the railing. "Do you smell that?"

Millie squeezed her eyes shut, praying the woman wouldn't stick her head around the corner and see her.

"It smells like barbecue. I'm starving."

"We should head upstairs," Kimberly said. "Hey, let's text Harper and invite her to join us. You know how much she loves barbecue."

"It wouldn't hurt to try. Stranger things have happened."

The women returned inside and Millie released the breath she was holding. It was clear neither woman knew exactly where Harper was hiding. How much Bryce knew was an entirely different matter, considering there were two wet towels hanging in the bathroom.

She tiptoed toward the railing. The ship's lifeboats were directly below. Millie began to feel lightheaded. The hatch on the one closest to Harper and Bryce's cabin was open, while the hatches on all the other lifeboats were closed.

Millie studied the distance between the deck and the top of the lifeboat. With a small amount of maneuvering and a deck chair, anyone could climb over the side and access the lifeboat, including Harper Rothshield.

She removed her cell phone and snapped a picture of the open hatch. Millie tapped the screen to enlarge the picture, but there wasn't much to see. Noting the location and lifeboat number, she stepped back inside and closed the door behind her.

Millie hesitated, listening for sounds of movement from Kimberly and Sierra's cabin. All was quiet, so she made her way to the exit door. She sucked in a breath and eased the door open. "Joy."

Joy appeared. "Oh my gosh. The women in the cabin next door showed up. At first, I thought this was their cabin and almost freaked out." Joy began babbling.

Millie nudged the delivery cart. "Can you move the cart so I can get out of here?"

"Yeah. Sorry." Joy wheeled it out of the way.

Millie stepped into the hall and pulled the door shut behind her.

"I'm not very good at this covert operation stuff," Joy said.

"Hold up." Millie did a timeout. "At the risk of sticking my nose in where it doesn't belong, which seems to be a bad habit of mine, rumor has it you got kicked out of the UK for being a spy."

"It was all a misunderstanding. That was my roommate. We were under surveillance. I had no idea she was a spy. Looking back, she did some weird stuff while we lived together, but who am I to judge?"

"So you're not a spy?"

"Nope, although it sounds exciting. It's a good thing I saw everything I wanted while I was over there because I'm pretty sure they're not going to let me come back," Joy said. "Guilt by association and all that."

"Some of it must've rubbed off on you because you made sure I didn't get busted and I might have figured out where our missing passenger is hiding out."

"That chick Harper something? Donovan and I were hanging out the other night, and he mentioned her name." Joy swirled her finger next to her forehead. "She sounds a little unbalanced."

"More like a lot. I think she's been in this cabin recently. Both bath towels are wet and there was a woman's shaver inside the shower."

Joy blinked rapidly. "Why isn't she staying in her cabin?"

"I wish I knew. She's gone on some sort of I'm-going-to-trash-a-cruise-ship rampage. She skipped out of rehab, booked this cruise last minute and then went berserk after her boyfriend started flirting with someone in the nightclub the first night of the cruise," Millie said. "And she doesn't like me."

"Doesn't like you?"

"She accused me of calling her a liar." Millie's phone chimed. It was a message from an unknown number.

"Great." Millie sucked in a breath. "It appears Harper has my cell phone number."

"How did she get that?" Joy asked.

"I don't know but I imagine if there's a will, there's a way."

"Good luck tracking her down, Millie. If you need another lookout, give me a call," Joy said. "I would even be up for a foot pursuit. I used to run mini marathons."

"Mini marathons? I can see that coming in handy," Millie said. "Thanks for the offer."

"Either way, I would love to help you catch this passenger before she does something else."

Millie read the text a second time. "Unfortunately, I think it's too late."

Chapter 13

Millie read the text aloud. "You'll never find me. Scooter number two is toast."

"Do you think this woman somehow knows you were snooping around?" Joy asked.

"It's possible." Millie thought about the lifeboat directly below Harper's cabin and the fact the top hatch was open. "She could've seen me standing out on her balcony."

"If she went ashore, the gangway security would know," Joy said.

"True." Millie thanked her friend again and parted ways with Joy near the bank of elevators, taking the nearest set of stairs to the lower deck.

A handful of passengers passed through the security checkpoints, both entering and exiting the ship. Millie found Suharto processing the passengers who were returning and waited until he was free.

"Hello, Millie. How is your day going?"

"It could be worse, although that's up for debate as soon as I figure a few things out," Millie said. "I was wondering if you could check to see if Harper Rothshield exited the ship."

"Dave Patterson phoned here a short time ago, asking the same question. She has not gotten off."

"I hate to bother you, but could you please check again?"

"Of course." Suharto tapped the monitor. "She hasn't gotten off the ship."

"Which means if she saw me, she wasn't standing on the dock," Millie murmured.

"What did you say?"

Millie waved dismissively. "Nothing. I'm talking to myself."

"I set up an alert. If she attempts to leave the ship, we'll be notified per Patterson's instructions."

Millie thanked him and swung by the laundry center. Despite all the bad news, there was a sliver of a silver lining. According to Rahul, the passenger's scooter had been repaired and returned to its owner.

"Is Sharky around?"

"No, Miss Millie. He was here earlier to retrieve the scooter. He is not in a good mood."

"Why?"

"His scooter has gone missing."

A sinking feeling settled in the pit of Millie's stomach. "Sharky's scooter—the Flamethrower—is missing?"

"Correct, and he is not happy."

"He loves that scooter." Millie thanked him for the update and trekked to the maintenance office.

The lights were off and the door was locked. She tried radioing Sharky, but there was no answer.

Her next call was to the security office. Dave Patterson had not yet returned. She needed someone to check the lifeboat closest to Harper's cabin. Patterson was gone and Sharky wasn't responding, which left only one other person who might be able to help.

Millie reached the bridge and found Nic, along with First Officer Craig McMasters, seated at the conference table. It was filled with stacks of papers, spread from end to end.

"Hello, Millie."

"Hey, Nic. I'm sorry to bother you, but I need help."

Nic shifted, giving his wife his full attention. "What is it?"

"We need someone to search lifeboat number eight."

“Search the lifeboat? Why?”

“The hatch is open, and I think the missing passenger might be hiding out inside.” She hurried on. “At the risk of incriminating myself, I would rather not explain why, but I think the sooner you have it searched, the better.”

“Sharky can get someone over there,” McMasters said.

“He’s not answering my calls. I think he...has his hands full.”

“Bauer is head of maintenance,” Nic said. “I’ll have him check it out.”

“Great.” Millie shifted her feet, waiting for him to make the call.

“Is there something else?”

“No.”

Nic slid the papers aside. “You want me to call him right now?”

“If at all possible.”

"I'll see what I can do." Nic made the call, quickly locating Frank Bauer, who assured him he would look into it.

Millie waited until he was done. "Thank you. I knew you could help. There is one more thing. I received this random text." She handed her husband her cell phone. "Rahul told me Sharky's scooter is missing. It appears Rothshield found a way to sneak into the crew's quarters."

She knew the exact second he finished the text by the grim expression on his face. "This woman is a threat to passengers and crew. Patterson is returning soon. I'll meet with him and the security staff as soon as possible." Nic handed the phone back. "Are you going to tell us how you were tipped off our missing passenger might be hiding out in the lifeboat?"

"Maybe…later." Millie began backing toward the door. "I need to run. Thanks again." She hurried out before Nic could stop her, praying that if

Harper was hiding in the lifeboat, she would be found.

Like clockwork, Millie hosted her events, including a VIP pampering party for the cruise line's diamond elites, followed by a meeting with the entertainment staff to go over the evening's headliner show.

Danielle popped in for the first Adventures at Eight with Andy taping, highlighting several of the upcoming activities and chatting about the ports. They wrapped it up and exited the recording studio.

"How did your fact-finding mission go?"

Millie glanced around and lowered her voice. "I believe Harper has been inside her cabin as recently as this morning. I found a woman's shaver in the shower. The two bath towels next to it were wet. I might have stumbled upon a clue and figured out where she's been hiding."

"Down in the crew quarters."

“Close.” Millie told her how she’d noticed the hatch was open on the lifeboat directly below Harper and Bryce’s cabin.

“That’s crazy.”

“I also overheard her friends talking out on their balcony. They have no idea where she is.”

“One step away from being committed to a mental health hospital would be my guess,” Danielle said. “Why on earth would she hide in a lifeboat when she has a comfy cozy cabin nearby?”

“Because she’s trying to punish her boyfriend, Bryce. You’ve got me, other than she’s mentally unstable. The good news is the passenger’s scooter has been repaired.”

Millie’s radio went off. It was Sharky. “Millie, are you there?”

“Go ahead Sharky.”

“Where are you?”

"With Danielle, standing outside the recording studio."

"I'm with Frank Bauer down on deck four portside, midship. Can you meet us there?"

"I'm on my way." Millie clipped her radio to her belt. "Ten bucks says the maintenance guys found something interesting in the lifeboat that I asked them to check."

Danielle pursed her lips. "I wish I could go with you, but I'm hosting a port talk in the theater. Fill me in on what happens."

Millie promised she would and made a mad dash for the lifeboat staging area.

Sharky spotted her first and began making his way toward her.

"Well? Did you find her hiding in the lifeboat?"

"Nope, but someone has been in there. Check it out." Sharky stepped into the narrow corridor which led to a solid steel door. The lifeboats were on the other side.

A ladder was propped against one of them, with Bauer perched on the top rung. "Hey, Millie. Does this look familiar?" Frank tossed her a sweatshirt.

Millie held it up. "It looks like the same hoodie the person who stole the passenger's scooter was wearing."

"There's more," Sharky said.

Frank held up a pair of binoculars, followed by a trash bag filled with empty wrappers and drink cups. There were also strips of a plain white bedsheet identical to the material Harper had used for her toga. "The boat is a mess. Whoever was in here trashed it."

"Harper might not be the tidiest person," Millie sighed.

"We're padlocking the hatches, at least until we can find the woman."

Millie's eyes traveled to the upper deck and Harper's balcony. She had been nearby the entire time. Where would she go if she was locked out of the lifeboats?

Patterson was most likely monitoring her keycard activity, but then maybe she hadn't accessed her cabin via the corridor. Maybe she'd been monitoring Bryce's activities from directly below and gone in via the slider when she knew he wasn't around.

Millie struggled to remember if the balcony door had been locked. She'd been in such a hurry to hide she couldn't remember. Either way, Millie was convinced Harper *had* been in her cabin at some point in time.

"Patterson is on his way back," Frank said. "I'll turn all of this over to him and he can handle it from there."

Sharky waited for Frank to secure the hatch, gather up his tools and leave. "You have a sharp eye, Millie. How did you figure out that chick was hiding in the lifeboat?"

Millie jabbed her finger toward Harper and Bryce's balcony. "I was up there having a look around and noticed the hatch was open. I can't even imagine how claustrophobic it was inside there." The thought of the cramped, dark space made her stomach churn.

"She'll get caught," Sharky predicted. "It's a good thing I was able to fix the passenger's scooter. If not, we would be adding it to the charges she's racking up. Damages at the nightclub, extra labor and supplies to sanitize and refill the pool. She broke the seal on the hatch so that will need to be repaired. You have to wonder what makes her tick."

Sharky fell into step as they made their way back inside. "Do you have any big plans or time off scheduled?"

"No. I was planning on heading ashore when we reached Curacao, but now that Andy's on emergency medical leave, I don't see that happening."

"How's he doing?"

"I don't know. I need to give him a call."

"Tell him we're thinking about him." Sharky turned to go, and Millie stopped him. "Rahul said your scooter went missing."

"Yeah. I parked it outside the office last night. Reef said he used it once but left it in the same spot. I'm sure one of the clowns in maintenance is messing with me again. It better turn up soon, or I'll start knocking some heads together."

"I hate to be the bearer of bad news, but I got an odd text earlier and I think it might be about your scooter." Millie pulled up the text and handed her phone to Sharky.

He made a choking sound. "The witch stole my scooter."

"It would appear so, which means she's found a way to sneak into the crew-only deck areas."

"Making her even more of a loose cannon."

"I was thinking the same thing. Nic is aware of what's going on and plans to meet with the security staff soon." After Sharky left, Millie dialed Andy's cell phone. She was almost certain it would go to voicemail, but was surprised when he picked up.

"Hello, Millie," Andy's voice boomed. "Cat and I were just talking about you. Danielle sent a video of the parade. You did a bang-up job."

"All because you laid the groundwork for me."

"How is it going? Are you keeping up with the extra workload?"

"Yes, thanks to your awesome staff, it's going better than expected. As far as the passenger who is hiding out and wreaking havoc. Not so good."

"Passenger hiding out? Did someone not leave during the last voyage and is doing a back-to-back for free?"

"Not even close. It's a long story and I don't want to bore you with the details. How are you doing?" Millie asked.

"The doctors have scheduled all sorts of tests."

"Are they leaning toward making a diagnosis?"

"I...maybe. Let's say if they confirm their suspicions, I might have to make some changes."

Millie's heart plummeted and she could feel her throat clog. She couldn't lose Andy. He was her friend, her mentor. "Changes?"

"I would rather wait until I have all the information, Millie. Cat and I agree I'm in good hands and have an excellent team trying to get to the bottom of it," Andy said. "The good news is I'll be back for the next voyage."

"I like the sounds of that."

“Cat would like to say hello.”

“Take care Andy.” Millie choked out the rest of the words. “We miss you.”

“I miss you too. Thank you for covering for me. I know you’re doing a good job. Here’s Cat.”

Millie dabbed at her eyes, overcome with emotion and missing her friends.

“Hey, Millie.”

“Hey, Cat. How are you?”

“Stressed. Tired. Andy’s not admitting to it, but he’s been through a lot.”

“I bet. I’m sorry to bother you. We’re all worried and everyone has been asking.”

“I wish we had more information. The doctor promises he’ll have something soon. There are only a few more tests to run. He’s going to put a rush on the results because he knows we don’t have a lot of time.”

"Half the battle is having faith in the medical team."

"It is," Cat agreed. "We know you're praying for us and we appreciate it. Please tell everyone we miss them—Annette, Danielle, Donovan."

"I will. Take care Cat. If you need anything, anything at all, please let me know." Millie wished them well and, after hanging up, she stood near the railing, struggling to compose herself. Andy and Cat were like family. Regardless of how he tried to sound nonchalant, she could hear the concern in her friend's voice.

She said a small prayer for them, squared her shoulders and threw herself into her next event.

The hours flew by and by dinnertime, most passengers had found their way back on board.

Millie briefly wondered if Patterson and his team had any luck tracking Harper down.

Knowing the head of security, she was certain he was probably having someone monitor the surveillance cameras at all times, yet even if they spotted the troublesome woman, by the time they arrived at that location, there was a good chance she would be long gone.

Millie ran backstage near the dinner hour to check on the headliner show—a medley of entertainers—the magician, comedian, the singers and dancers, were all on tap for the evening's entertainment.

A jumble of voices coming from the rear staging area grew louder as Millie drew closer. Blackjack Blaze, the self-proclaimed "Jack of All Trades," part magician, part ventriloquist and part comedian, all rolled into one, stood front and center, squaring off against Tara Daughtery, one of the ship's dancers.

"What's going on?"

"My assistant Monique is ill. I need someone to fill in for my magic act. Tara is the only female who isn't in the main show. She's the perfect size, yet she's refusing to help."

"What's wrong with Monique?" Millie asked. "Perhaps it's nerves."

"She's throwing up and has a fever," Blaze said bluntly.

"I see. We'll be right back." Millie escorted Tara into Andy's office and closed the door behind them. "You're not in tonight's dance number."

"No." Tara winced as she performed a step-touch. "I tripped during an earlier practice and my ankle is swelling."

"And you don't want to work with Blackjack Blaze?" Millie asked.

Tara shook her head and lowered her gaze.

"Because..."

"He's creepy. Those dark eyes. What if he saws me in half?" Tara asked.

Millie had gotten a similar impression. There was something slightly unnerving about him. "Don't worry about it. I'll figure something out. In the meantime, I want you to run down to medical and have them check your ankle."

"I will." Tara, appearing immensely relieved, thanked Millie and limped out of the office.

Millie stared at Andy's framed photo on the wall. "I'm taking one for the team, Andy. You will never be able to say I didn't take one for the team. This is shaping up to be one long night."

Chapter 14

"I look ridiculous." Millie grimaced as she tugged on the neckline of the sequined swimsuit. "I'm swimming in it, literally. Isn't there something in the wardrobe closet that would better suit someone of my stature and shape?"

"All you need is a cover." Alison snagged a neon pink velvet cape from the rack and held it up. "This is a perfect match and won't drag on the floor."

Millie wrinkled her nose. "No way. I'll draw attention like a masked bank robber holding a gun and bag of cash in front of a cop shop."

Alison hung the pink number back on the rack and grabbed a multi-colored, mini-halter, hip-hugging fluorescent wraparound dress.

"Ack." Millie made a slicing motion across her neck. "The colors are burning my retinas."

"It also glows in the dark."

"We're running out of time." Millie plucked at the swimsuit. "Find me a cover, any cover."

Alison handed her a light wrap.

Millie gave it the once-over and wrapped it around her lower half. "This will have to do."

"You look great. The wrap flows, giving the illusion you're floating across the stage."

"Floating, not dragging and dusting the floor at the same time."

Blackjack appeared. "Danielle is wrapping up introductions. It's showtime."

"What magic act are you performing again?" Millie's anxiety ramped up several notches. Her concern over the fact Blackjack had refused to elaborate on how she would be involved was increasing exponentially.

Unfortunately, it was too late to back out now. The audience began applauding.

Danielle hurried off the stage. “You’re up. You look great, Millie.”

“Thanks.” Millie forced herself to relax, praying she wouldn’t embarrass herself as she lifted the bottom of the wrap and accompanied Blackjack on stage.

“Good evening, ladies and gentlemen, and welcome. I’m Blackjack Blaze, the Jack-of-all-trades. For those of you who’ve been hiding in your cabin during this voyage, please allow me the great pleasure of introducing my assistant and your cruise director, Millie Armati.”

The crowd applauded and Millie gritted her teeth beneath her pasted-on smile.

“I think we can all agree the theme of a cruise, other than rest and relaxation, is the sun, sea and sand, particularly on these fabulous Caribbean voyages.”

The curtain behind them opened, revealing a beach scene, complete with piles of powdery white sand, a faux sun dangling from a nearly invisible rope with a sea of blue skies behind it.

Blaze grasped her hand and led Millie toward the props. "Let's pretend Millie's spent a day at one of Bonaire's beautiful beaches." He tapped the top of the folding chair. "Have a seat."

"Dim the lights. My pale skin is going to blind you," Millie joked.

The crowd chuckled.

Blackjack ignored the comment, steadying Millie as she lowered onto the seafoam green folding chair. He handed her a book from the nearby table and a drink with a miniature umbrella sticking out of the top. "What a gorgeous day at the beach...sipping your fruity beverage and reading a good book."

Blackjack motioned to Millie.

"Uh. It is." Millie flipped the book open and pretended to sip the drink.

"But it's getting warm. It's time for a dip in the water." While Blackjack talked, a trio of stagehands rolled a clear tube-shaped tank of water onto the stage.

"You-you want me to get in there?" Millie tightened her grip on the book, gauging the depth of the water.

"It's time to cool off."

"The only way in is to dive from the rafters."

Blackjack held up a finger. "Not quite, although that would make a big splash."

Millie shot him an annoyed look, struggling to come up with a clever comeback.

The same crew brought out a spiral staircase, a prop from the Gem of the Sea's show.

Blackjack collected Millie's book and drink and set them on the table. "A dip is the perfect way to enjoy your day." He lowered his voice to barely above a whisper. "Ditch the skirt."

Millie unclipped her microphone and handed it to him. "No way. You're not paying me enough."

"You're the cruise director," Blackjack reminded her. "The show must go on."

Millie's jaw was clenched so tightly her temples were starting to throb. She held tight to the wrap, cautiously making her way up the spiral staircase.

She reached the top step and in one swift move, whipped the beach wrap off and tossed it in Blackjack's direction.

Someone catcalled, and Millie could feel her cheeks turn flaming red. She straddled the side of the tank and shot a furtive glance toward the audience.

"I'm asking for a raise," she muttered under her breath, right before cannonballing in. She sank down and then shot to the top, sputtering as she surfaced.

She glimpsed the crew and staff standing behind the curtain, their eyes wide as they watched her paddle around, struggling to keep her head above water.

It was a full house, all watching as Blackjack rambled on about how he was the greatest comedian / magician on the planet.

"Can we get on with the show?" Millie hollered. "I have a trivia contest in half an hour."

The crowd roared with laughter as she continued paddling.

Blackjack, with the help of the crewmembers who had wheeled the human aquarium and spiral staircase onto the stage, slowly spun Millie around in a full circle. "As you can see, our cruise director is completely submerged in this tank of water. Millie?" Blackjack held a hand to his ear. "Are you wet?"

"What do you think?"

More laughter.

"I think Millie has had sufficient time to cool off." Blackjack made his way to the top of the staircase. He knelt on the top step and extended a hand.

Millie was no longer flailing and could feel the base beneath her rising, pushing her toward the top. Instead of being cold and wet, she was dry...as dry as she was when she'd cannonballed in.

She snatched the wrap off the railing and slung it around her, tying it securely while Blackjack snapped his fingers, motioning to one of the crewmembers who handed him a beach towel. "Would you like this?"

"I don't know how you pulled it off, but I'm dry...as dry as I was before I got in."

With great flourish, Blackjack tossed the towel back to the man and led Millie down the steps. They circled the stage with the magician's hand tightly gripping hers as they paraded back and forth. "Sun, sand and sea and Millie as dry as she can be."

Blackjack and Millie took a bow as the crowd sprang to their feet. They began chanting her name. "Millie...Millie..."

Blackjack unclipped his microphone. "They adore you Millie. Perhaps you can help with the second show."

"Not on your life," she gritted out. "This was a one and done. You have an hour and a half to find someone else."

"Great job." Danielle stood waiting for them to exit the stage. "You aren't even wet," she marveled as she rubbed Millie's arm. "How did he do that?"

"I don't know. I was focusing on not drowning or losing the bathing suit. Blackjack is looking for someone for the next show. Maybe you should volunteer."

"No way." Danielle shook her head. "I would love to know how he did that, but not enough to put myself out there."

The entertainment staff crowded around, congratulating Millie while Danielle headed to the stage to end the show.

Millie gripped the bottom of the wrap and trekked into Andy's office. She shut the door and locked it before swapping out the costume for her uniform. By the time she finished, she found the theater was empty except for a handful of the cleaning crew who were collecting empty glasses and discarded napkins.

With minutes to spare, Millie made it to the trivia location and was greeted by several passengers who tracked her down to tell her how much they enjoyed Blackjack's part of the show.

Hours later, Millie trudged up to the nightclub, her last stop of the long day. Tahitian Nights was hopping, and the place was packed. She checked in with the bar staff and began heading home when her radio went off.

It was Sharky. "You still working?"

"Yeah. I'm finishing my shift. What's up?"

"Can you meet me in front of the spa?"

At first, Millie thought she had heard him wrong. "Did you say the spa?"

"Yeah. We found the Flamethrower."

Chapter 15

Millie's first clue something was terribly wrong was the fact the doors to the spa were wide open. As she drew closer, she noticed deep gouges in the glass and the decorative gold locks and handles that secured the spa doors were dangling.

Sharky paced while a small army of maintenance guys ran around inside. "Hey, Millie."

"What happened?"

"Someone stole my scooter, drove it up here, and used it as a battering ram to break down the door. Patterson is off for the night. Oscar is on his way." Sharky led Millie inside. "Watch your step. The floor is like an ice rink."

Millie stared at the shelves which, only hours earlier, had been filled with bottles of creams and lotions, natural scrubs and expensive oils, now broken and the contents smeared everywhere—the shelves, the walls, the floor.

"I'm pretty sure the hoodie hoodlum who stole the other scooter and drove it into the pool is behind this. She's probably ticked because we locked down her hiding spot."

Millie was almost afraid to ask. "Where's your scooter, the Flamethrower?"

"This way." Sharky trudged down the hall that led to the treatment rooms. He stopped when they reached the salt therapy steam room. "It's in there."

A blast of dry heat enveloped Millie as she stepped inside. Her eyes widened in horror when she noticed the Flamethrower lying on its side, sporting a busted taillight. "Your scooter is trashed."

Sharky grabbed a hand towel and pulled it upright. "Check out the front."

Fin's basket was smashed in, along with the front fender. The tires were flatter than pancakes and it looked as if a dump truck had run over the front half.

"This is awful. How did they steal it?"

"The keys are on a hook by the door. Someone must've accidentally left the door unlocked. She sneaked inside, grabbed the key and took it for a smash and grab joyride." Sharky kicked the flat front tire. "What is it with the scooters and joyriding?" he ranted.

"I don't know," Millie said. "It's easier for her to make her rounds destroying stuff?"

"It gets worse. Hang on." Sharky stuck his head in the hall and looked both ways. "Whoever it was also stole some emergency flares."

Millie sucked in a breath. "What could she possibly want with those?"

"Who knows?" Sharky shrugged. "To scare the daylights out of passengers and create chaos?"

Millie started to pace. "From day one she's been causing trouble, starting with making a scene down in the nightclub. She hijacked a passenger's scooter, took it for a joyride and drove it into the pool."

"She figured out how to turn the theater's emergency sprinklers on and now this. It makes you wonder when she sleeps." Sharky shook his head in disgust.

"During the day. My guess is she sleeps during the day so she can do her dirty work at night, when there aren't as many passengers or crewmembers around to catch her."

"So the flares are up next," Sharky said.

The sound of heavy footsteps grew louder. Oscar and a team of security guards appeared. "We have at least some of the surveillance footage. We can clearly see Sharky's scooter heading in this direction. I've forwarded a copy to the captain for review."

A maintenance crewmember rolled a large cart to the door while Sharky and some of the other workers carried the Flamethrower into the hall and hoisted it on top. "I can't wait until this chick is off the ship or gets taken down."

"Hang in there." Millie patted his shoulder. "The flares are a major concern. Hopefully, she's tuckered out from an evening of destruction, giving us time to regroup."

"We have extra men patrolling the ship," Oscar said. "The spa was also part of the extra patrol. She must have been watching for them and waited until they made their rounds to break in."

"We need to do something, and fast," Millie said. "I'm heading home and will find out what Nic thinks our next step should be."

By the time Millie arrived, her husband had finished his shift and joined her in the apartment.

"Our unstable cruiser is still at it."

"Unfortunately." Millie let out a low groan as she sank into the chair and kicked her shoes off. "Poor Sharky's scooter is in rough shape."

"We have to find this woman."

Millie shared her suspicions. "I think she sleeps during the day and is up all night wreaking havoc. Imagine what will happen if she sets off one of those flares." The thought that popped into her head was so horrifying she didn't dare voice it.

Nic did. "...a crowded nightclub, causing a panic and stampede," he said grimly.

"It's not out of the question, considering how this whole thing started when Harper caused a scene in the nightclub and was escorted out."

"We'll have to monitor the piano bar, Marseille Lounge, the nightclub, and implement mandatory searches at the door."

Millie followed her husband into the kitchen, watching as he removed a pack of deli meat and cheese slices from the fridge. "Oscar said he forwarded a copy of the surveillance video from the spa incident to you."

"He did. It doesn't show much, other than a hooded vandal busting down the spa doors and destroying the stuff inside."

"Whoever it was abandoned Sharky's scooter when they reached the salt therapy steam room. During their rampage, they busted the fender, broke the taillight, and flattened the tires. He'll be lucky if he can fix it."

"I'm not surprised, considering how they used it to break in."

"Do you mind if I take a look at the video? Maybe I can pick up on something the others may have missed."

"Be my guest. It's in my email."

While Nic fixed a snack, Millie settled in front of the computer. She logged into the company's system and opened Nic's account. The email and attachment from the security department was at the top.

She grew quiet as she watched the grainy image of the spa lobby and doors. A few seconds in, she could see Sharky's scooter, the red flame on the side, catching the light as it zipped along the corridor.

The hooded driver hunched down as they came to an abrupt halt. The vandal hopped off and leaned in, scoping out the door locks.

Moments later, they climbed back on and made a U-turn. The scooter disappeared and then reappeared, this time moving at an even faster clip.

Bam! Millie flinched as the scooter ran smack-dab into the center of the doors. The doors shook but held. The driver did another U-turn and came at them again.

The doors started to give and she could see the lockset loosening.

After looping around a third time, the scooter disappeared and then reappeared as it raced down the hall and rammed into the glass doors. The doors flew open, and the scooter cruised right on in.

The first recording ended. A second one started to play. It was from a different camera, a different angle, recording from inside the spa. The hooded hoodlum snatched up a pair of glass bottles and flung them at the wall.

They shattered on impact, and colored liquid ran down the walls, spilling onto the floor. Methodically working their way from right to left, the vandal began smashing bottles, removing lids and squirting expensive spa products everywhere...on the walls, the shelves, the floor.

It seemed to go on forever but was only a matter of minutes before the vandal hopped back on and the scooter wobbled down the hall.

The recording ended. There wasn't a third. Millie returned to the main screen and forwarded the email and attachments to her inbox.

She clicked away from Nic's inbox and logged into her account. There were only a couple of messages from the staff, a question about the next port stop and a request for a schedule change.

There was also one from Blackjack. His message included a photo of the two of them taken during the show. Millie was climbing the spiral staircase, making her way toward the top of the dunk tank.

Nic wandered over, leaning in as he let out a catcall. "That is one sexy lady right there."

Millie could feel the tips of her ears burn as she stared at her bikini-clad body on stage, under bright lights and parading around in front of hundreds of people. "Believe me, if I had even an inkling of what I was getting myself into, I would've refused."

"You're a team player, an entertainer through and through. You would never let our guests down," Nic said. "I heard the applause, the laughter. Your performance was the highlight of the show."

Millie wagged her finger at him. "You're biased."

"Possibly." Nic gently kissed her lips.

"You're trying to distract me," Millie accused as she playfully nudged him.

"Guilty as charged." Nic winked at his wife. "It's a shame we won't be going to the beach. You could have borrowed the bathing suit for our date day tomorrow."

"Date day." Millie frowned.

"Don't you remember? We have a half day off when we reach Curacao," he reminded her.

"I thought...I figured with Andy on leave, it would be a no-go."

"You've been going nonstop since we left port." Nic pulled her into his arms. "You earned your half day off. So did I, and I intend for us to take full advantage of it. Besides, I have a special surprise planned."

Millie's eyes narrowed. "You know how I feel about surprises."

"Which typically involves Andy, not me," Nic pointed out.

"True. I'm sure the ship-sponsored excursions are already booked up. What about..."

Nic placed his finger against his wife's lips. "Give that inquiring mind of yours a break and trust me when I promise you that you're going to enjoy every minute of what I have planned."

"What if someone needs me?"

"The majority of the passengers will be off the ship. Curacao is a lovely island. I've checked the weather. It's going to be warm and sunny *and* Scout is going with us. Isn't that right, buddy?"

Scout, hearing his name, pounced on Millie's stockinged foot and pawed at her pantleg. "Did you hear that Scout? We get the day off."

Nic leaned in for a kiss. "We'll need to be one of the first ones off the ship so we should probably think about turning in." He grabbed her hand and began leading her toward the stairs. "About that sexy little bathing suit you were wearing earlier..."

Chapter 16

Nic and Millie were among the first off the ship after the security team announced the all-clear early the next morning. Scout, thrilled to be out in the fresh air, ran circles around his stroller, eager to take it all in.

Nic glanced at his watch. "I need to send a quick text."

Millie playfully peered over his shoulder. "Who are you texting?"

"You'll find out soon enough." Nic shielded the screen. His phone pinged seconds later. "I love it when a plan comes together. Your surprise is eagerly awaiting our arrival."

Millie could see passengers turning right as they exited the gangway, meandering along the sidewalk past a variety of vendors who were hawking their wares. "Where is everyone going? We might be missing something awesome over that way."

Nic chuckled. "We'll be visiting the area *after* my surprise. I see the taxis on the other side of the security checkpoint. Let's go."

While Nic negotiated the rate, Millie folded Scout's stroller and slid it into the trunk. She placed the pup on the seat. He promptly trampled over the top of her, impatiently waiting for Nic and the driver to join them.

Finally, they were on their way. Back and forth he went, racing from window to window as their taxi cruised along the shoreline.

"You're the first passenger I've ever had who brought a dog ashore," the driver said. "Did you sneak him on?"

"The captain gave us special permission to bring him on board," Nic said.

"That's cool." The driver checked for traffic before continuing. "I've never been on a cruise before. Your ship looks pretty luxurious. How many restaurants are there?"

Millie rattled off the number of restaurants and lounges.

"Whoa. There must be a lot of people working on your ship."

"Quite a few," Nic agreed.

"I gotta say, I drive a lot of cruise ship passengers around. Some of them, they complain about this or that but I've never heard anyone complain about Siren of the Seas, so it must be a good one."

Nic winked at his wife. "Siren of the Seas is one of the best."

"Tell us about the island," Millie said. "What are the top things we shouldn't miss?"

"You gotta check out the swinging bridge."

"Swinging bridge," she echoed.

“We call her the Swinging Old Lady. She’s a floating bridge connecting Otrobanda and Punda.”

“How interesting. What keeps it from sinking?”

“Pontoon boats are holding it up. It swings to the side to let ships in and out of the bay. If you’re lucky enough to be standing on it when it opens, you get a free ride,” the driver said.

“Nic.” Millie squeezed her husband’s hand. “We need to check it out.”

“Don’t miss the Rif Fort. It’s right next door.”

“We’ll be visiting both before we head back to the ship,” Nic promised his wife.

Near the outskirts of town, their driver turned inland. They zigged and zagged along the side streets, through several neighborhoods, weaving back and forth so many times Millie was no longer sure which direction they were heading.

The car rounded a bend, and a bay came into view. The road dead-ended in front of a set of wrought-iron gates. A sign marked *ABC Animal Sanctuary* was prominently displayed.

"This is a great place. I brought my parrot here a couple of weeks ago because he wasn't eating. They figured out what was wrong with him and he's back to his old self. The sanctuary was shut down for over a year before new owners bought the place, cleaned it up, and now they're back in business." Their driver glanced in the rearview mirror. "Are you taking your dog there for a checkup?"

"No. We're here to visit," Nic said. "The new owners are friends of ours."

"I can't remember the woman's name. She's a real sweet lady. I think she told me she was from Indonesia. Young gal. Anyway, tell her Jose said 'hi' and Frankie, my parrot, is doing much better."

"I will." Nic waited for the taxi to pull alongside the curb. He climbed out and grabbed Scout, who was teetering on the edge of the seat, mapping out his escape plan. "Hang on there, Scout. We'll never find you if you get lost."

Jose set the stroller on the curb and joined Nic to settle the cab fare. Meanwhile, Millie adjusted the stroller's side rails, giving Scout some extra room to explore while ensuring he wouldn't be able to sneak out.

The pup placed his paws on the padded bar, his button nose turned toward the light ocean breeze, and his ears perked up.

"I wonder what Scout will think when he sees all the different animals." Millie patted his head. "Look at that adorable little face. He doesn't know what to do."

"I thought he might have fun." Nic steered the stroller through the gate and Millie fell into step. "You told the driver the owners were friends."

"They are."

"Close friends?" Millie persisted.

Nic cast her a side glance. "That busy little brain of yours never stops."

"Never."

They reached the ticket booth, and the woman behind the plexiglass greeted them. "Welcome to ABC Animal Sanctuary."

"Thank you."

"Is it just the two of you?"

"Yes, and our pup, Scout."

"Scout gets in free. It will be thirty dollars for two tickets."

Nic handed the woman his card. She rang up the sale. He signed the slip and slid it back across the counter. "We're here to see the owners. They're expecting us."

The woman plucked a sticky note off the counter. "Are you Captain Armati?"

"I am."

"I wasn't supposed to charge you."

"Consider it a donation to a good cause," Nic said.

"I'll radio the owners to let them know you're here." The cashier stepped away from the counter and Nic began talking. "Have you guessed who it is yet?"

"Jose said the young woman was from Indonesia." Millie pressed a hand to her chest. "Nadia. Is it Nadia and Regan?"

"It is," Nic beamed.

"I thought...they live on Saint-Martin. What are they doing here? Did they sell their gorgeous resort?"

Nic held up a hand. "I don't know all the details. Regan told me some time back he and Nadia were considering investing in another property. He called me out of the blue the other day and told me they were here in Curacao. I told him the island was one of our port stops, and he invited us to stop by."

"This is so exciting." Millie clapped her hands. "We haven't seen Nadia and Regan in ages."

A golf cart appeared with Regan behind the wheel and a smiling Nadia at his side. They circled around and hopped out, with everyone talking at once. Millie hugged her friends. "What are you doing in Curacao?"

"Things were running a little too smoothly at Grand Bay Beach Club and my ambitious wife decided we needed to shake things up," Regan teased.

"Stop." Nadia nudged her husband. "A friend of mine told me about this place, how the sanctuary had shut down and desperately needed new owners. I convinced Regan to fly down here to check it out."

"The next thing I know, we were signing on the dotted line."

"It's only an hour and a half flight from Saint-Martin," Nadia explained. "We've almost finished renovating the small cottage we've been living in. It has a spectacular view of the water. Our plan is to spend half the year living here and the other half at the resort."

"The best of both worlds," Nic said. "Do you have time to give us a tour?"

"Absolutely." Regan motioned to the four-seater golf cart. "We even have room for Scout's stroller in the back." With some quick rearranging, the four of them and Scout were soon on their way.

The tour started near the check-in booth, followed by a visit to the rehabilitation wing, and a brief stop by the training center where a class was in session.

"This place is bigger than it looks from the road," Millie said.

"Much bigger, but well laid out." Regan eased off the pedal and pulled into an empty parking spot. "Scout will like this stop the best. We offer pet boarding for the islanders. It helps generate some extra income."

"It makes sense to diversify your income streams," Millie said. "You have a very smart setup."

"We keep busy. The marina area is my favorite," Nadia said. "We would show you our cozy cottage, but it's a mess right now."

"Maybe next time," Millie said.

Regan and Nadia greeted the worker behind the reception desk as they led their friends toward the back. "We keep our feline guests on this side." Nadia opened a door marked *The Cool Cats Hotel.*

Scout let out an excited yip, his small body trembling as the door swung open. The large room was filled with cats...lounging on beds, sprawled out on various carpeted cat trees, perched on top of cardboard boxes.

A pair of kittens wrestled on the floor.

"Scout doesn't know what to think." Millie cautiously placed him on the floor. He pressed against her, warily watching the furry felines.

A calico cat sauntered over, eyeing him curiously.

"Someone wants to be friends," Millie said.

Scout's ears flattened, his small black nose wiggling ninety miles an hour. The cat inched closer while the pup held his ground.

Deeming the dog a non-threat, the cat batted at him. Scout batted back.

"Chloe is one of our friendliest cats," Regan explained.

It was as if Chloe was sending the pup some sort of signal because she turned to go and Scout followed her. The kittens, who had been tussling on the floor, pranced over and began playing with him while several others crowded around.

"I'll keep an eye on Scout if you want to check out the rest of the boarding area," the worker said.

"That's so sweet of you to offer, Tanya, but we need to keep moving and I think Scout will enjoy meeting our visiting pups as well," Nadia said.

Scout said goodbye to his new friends, and they headed across the hall to the door marked *Dogs at Play*.

Scout eagerly trotted into the room. There were big dogs, little dogs, poodles, labradoodles, and even a pup who could have been his twin.

Pure joy filled Scout's face as he raced around the room, meeting and greeting the other dogs. He played fetch with the worker and several other pups.

"We should keep moving." Nic reluctantly consulted his watch.

Nadia touched his arm. "We can leave Scout here to play."

"Absolutely." The worker who was throwing the ball gave Scout a pat on the head. "All of these dogs are a level one. He'll be fine hanging out with us until you're ready to pick him up."

"Level one?" Millie asked.

"Non-aggressive or non-dominant dogs are allowed to roam freely in the play area. In other words, they play well together," Regan said.

"We have a few who are afraid or the owners are not one hundred percent sure how they'll interact with strangers and other dogs," Nadia added. "We spend one-on-one time with them in a controlled environment where they feel safe."

Millie knelt on the floor and called Scout to her side. "Would you like to stay and play?"

Scout, his tiny pink tongue hanging from his mouth, pranced excitedly.

"I think that's a 'yes.'"

Nadia promised they would return, and the couples continued their tour. There was a visitor center, an interactive aquarium, a cafeteria and even a bird sanctuary.

"You must love it here," Millie said.

"It's wonderful, so different from the resort. Instead of working with people, we work with animals," Regan said.

"We don't get nearly as many complaints," Nadia joked.

It was clear the couple had found their passion by the excitement in their voices and plans for the future.

They reached the back of the property and a large lagoon that spilled into the ocean. A pair of dolphins frolicked nearby and, upon spotting them, cruised over.

"We're even dipping our toes into the rehabilitation end of the business," Regan said. "Daisy is our first patient. We suspect she tangled with a boat propeller and her fin got nicked. It's healing nicely and soon she'll be back out in the wild."

"I love dolphins. Nic and I visited the aquarium on the other side of the island a while back. Are you working with them?"

"We are. They contact us if they come across an animal in distress."

Millie perched on the edge of the wall and Daisy cruised past, close enough for her to run a hand along her side. "She's beautiful."

All too soon, the tour ended. They circled back to grab Scout, and a taxi was waiting near the gate to take them to the port.

Sudden tears filled Millie's eyes as she said goodbye to her friends. "It was so good to catch up."

"Perhaps next time, you can carve time out of your busy schedule and let us host lunch on board the ship," Nic suggested.

"We would love to." Nadia squeezed Millie's hand. "Married life certainly agrees with you. I swear you look younger every time I see you."

"It's all because of Nic," Millie said. "He's the best thing that ever happened to me."

With a fond farewell, the couple and Scout were on their way.

The driver dropped them off near Queen Emma's swinging bridge, and they meandered from one side to the other while Scout, tuckered out from making new friends, napped in his stroller.

Midway back across, a boat began making its way out of the bay. The couple stayed on for the ride and snapped selfies with the cruise ship as their backdrop.

The bridge returned to its original position, and the couple strolled toward the nearby fort.

"I don't know about you, but I'm starving." Millie sniffed appreciatively, catching the faint aroma of garlic and grilling meat.

"Let's check out Rif Fort first," Nic suggested. "It won't take long and then I have a special place picked out for our early lunch."

They passed through the entrance and stopped to read the plaque. "How interesting. I love UNESCO sites," Millie said.

"The former fort, with walls almost a foot thick, contained 56 cannons at one time. It was also used as police headquarters, a prison, and possibly even a brothel," Nic said.

They snapped a few more pictures before Nic led her up a set of side stairs to a restaurant overlooking the harbor with Siren of the Seas as the backdrop.

Millie chose grilled fish, lemon potatoes and grilled asparagus for lunch, while Nic dined on ribs, a baked potato, and corn on the cob.

They ordered a small dish of salmon for Scout, who gobbled up his goodies.

Eager to try a local dish, they ordered stroopwafel, a thin, round waffle cookie filled with caramel. Their server brought two spoons and a dish of vanilla ice cream to go along with it.

Finally, it was time to head back to the ship. The couple reluctantly gathered up their belongings for the short trek along the water and leisurely stroll back to the ship.

Millie linked arms with Nic. "Thank you for a wonderful date day."

"It was time off that was much needed and well-deserved," Nic said. "It was also nice to catch up with Regan and Nadia."

"It was," Millie said. "I feel as if I've recharged my batteries and nothing can get me down."

Little did Millie know that things were going to heat up...heat up a whole lot more as far as Harper Rothshield was concerned, and she would be right in the thick of it.

Chapter 17

The couple passed through the security checkpoint and found Patterson, along with several of the security staff, gathered near the passenger gangway.

"Something's going on," Millie said.

Nic glanced at his cell phone. "It can't be too serious. No one has called."

Patterson caught Nic's eye and made his way over. "How was your time off?"

"Wonderful," Millie said. "We caught up with some old friends. Scout made *new* friends, and we even had time to explore the port area."

"What's going on?" Nic motioned toward the security guards.

"I have some good news and some bad news. The good news is we tracked Harper Rothshield down."

"That is good news."

"The bad news is, she got off the ship before we were able to stop her. She blended in with a tour group and by the time the system alerted security that her card had been used, she had already slipped through."

"She's off the ship now," Nic clarified.

"Yes, sir."

"Which means we'll be watching for her and nab her when she tries to get back on," Millie said.

"That's the plan."

Feeling somewhat relieved the woman who had caused so much trouble for the ship and crew was actually off, Millie headed home to swap out her street clothes for her work uniform.

She started her midday work schedule by meeting with several of the entertainment staff to iron out a few minor issues. Millie swung by the spa to see how they were faring after she finished. The doors were locked so she tapped lightly on the window until an employee noticed her and let her in.

"How is it going?"

"It's a mess. We're trying to tally the damages along with track down passengers who booked treatments. Camille is fit to be tied." The woman rubbed her thumb and index finger together. "The break-in is costing the spa big bucks in damages and lost revenue."

"I bet." Millie glanced over her shoulder. "Is Camille around?"

"She's in the back with Stephen Chow, our acupuncturist. The vandal destroyed some of his equipment while they were at it."

"How awful."

"It's a bummer. Port days are some of our busiest days, with passengers taking advantage of the spa specials."

"No treatment equals no tip. I'm sorry you're dealing with this." Millie thanked the woman, wished her luck and made her way down the hall.

She paused in front of Stephen Chow's consulting room and could hear low voices. Camille and Chow were deep in conversation. Not wanting to interrupt, she continued walking until she reached the steam room where Sharky's scooter had been found before finally exiting through the fitness center.

Millie grabbed her radio and stepped off to the side. "Hey, Sharky."

"Go ahead, Millie."

"How's the Flamethrower?"

"It's back in business, but it ain't pretty. Where are you?"

"I just left the spa. They're still cleaning up."

"If you have time, swing by the recycling center. I found something you might be interested in."

"I'm on my way." Millie took the closest stairs all the way down, until she crossed over to the crew-only area. She reached the recycling center and found Sharky standing near the massive bins.

The Flamethrower was parked nearby. Sharky wasn't kidding. Duct tape held the front fender in place. The seat was torn with even more duct tape wrapped around it. Fin's basket was crumpled, although she could tell someone had tried fixing it.

The broken taillight was gone, and a bare bulb protruded out.

Sharky hustled over. "It's a good thing that chick got off the ship because if I had gotten my hands on her, I would've strangled her."

"I'm sure once Patterson detains her, he'll put her under cabin arrest."

"Or throw her in jail with only bread and water."

"Sharky," Millie chided. "What if she's mentally unstable and unable to control her urges? From what I was told, she skipped out of a rehab center and was attempting to get straightened out by going cold turkey."

"She failed miserably. I say good riddance. Patterson should refuse to let her back on."

"We aren't one hundred percent certain she's behind the vandalism, theft, destruction and chaos."

"Tracking down evidence is merely a formality and we both know it," Sharky said. "That wasn't why I called you down here." He reached into his pocket and pulled out a small round disc, roughly the size of a quarter. "Check this out."

"What is it?"

"A magnetic tracking tag." Sharky pressed it against the metal basket. "I found it stuck to the Flamethrower's battery cover."

"It's not yours?" Millie asked.

"Nope. It doesn't belong to Reef or anyone else from the maintenance department, which leads me to believe whoever stole my scooter lost it during their rampage."

Millie brightened. "Sweet. Track down the owner and we can nail Harper or whoever it is."

"Only if he, she, or they placed it in lost mode. If the owner doesn't put it in lost mode, there's no way to track them down," Sharky said. "I'm turning it over to Patterson, but again, it won't help if the tag isn't activated."

"Why would she need this on board the ship?"

Sharky shrugged. "I've seen them on keyrings and other stuff you want to keep track of."

A horrifying thought occurred to Millie. "What if she planned to track someone or something?"

"Could be. I wouldn't put anything past the crazy lady."

Millie headed out, mulling over Sharky's find. Had the woman planned to place the tracking device somewhere on board the ship after tearing the spa apart? If so, she was a busy woman—busy causing all sorts of trouble. To be honest, it wouldn't hurt Millie's feelings if she didn't return, either.

*****

It was late afternoon by the time Millie arrived at the library to host her holiday craft class.

Amit, who had offered to help, showed up with a cart filled with goodies not long after. "What are we making?" she asked, eyeing the cart with interest.

"Turkey treats—or reindeer, depending on what guests decide to create. They look a lot alike." Amit grabbed a bag of rice crispy treats and held them up. "These make the perfect base."

"I love rice crispy treats." Millie helped him arrange the M&M's, candy corn, mini-marshmallows, bite-size Reese's peanut butter cups, pretzels, and other sweets on the table near the door.

The guests started to arrive, and Millie greeted them while Amit stood near the table, helping them gather their supplies.

She tracked down a small radio and soft Christmas music began playing in the background while the creatives worked. Millie made her rounds, admiring the cleverness of each creation.

"Are you going to make one, Miss Millie?"

Millie turned to find Amit standing nearby.

"I...I'm not very creative."

"It is easy. I will show you."

Not wanting to hurt her friend's feelings, Millie reluctantly placed one of the remaining rice crispy circles on a paper plate. She dabbed frosting on the back of a mini-marshmallow and stuck it on top. She added several more before copying someone else's idea of using an Almond Joy bar for the face.

She used a red M&M for the nose and then snipped a small strip of red licorice rope for the mouth. After adding two candy eyes, Millie proudly held up her reindeer. "I did it."

"See? You are very creative," Amit said. "It looks like a delicious, sweet treat."

"Almost too pretty to eat," she quipped.

The craft class ended and Millie snapped pictures of each attendee and their creation, promising to forward the pictures to the emails listed on the sign-in sheet. Amit and Millie made quick work of cleaning up with minutes to spare before it was time to host bingo.

The crowds were light, which wasn't unusual considering the number of passengers who were still off the ship.

Millie spotted a familiar face coming toward her after the last round ended. It was Harper's friend, Kimberly. "Hello, Millie."

"Hello, Kimberly. Did you visit Curacao?"

Kimberly tapped the tip of her red nose. "Visited it, forgot my sunscreen and will now return home with a burnt nose as a souvenir."

Millie grinned. "You aren't the first and I'm sure you won't be the last."

Sierra waltzed over, flashing a wad of cash. "I won a hundred bucks."

"Congratulations." Millie changed the subject. "Have you heard from Harper?"

"Yes. She's been blowing our cell phones up. She got off the ship. I'm kinda surprised. I figured the ship's security guards would've stopped her."

"What about Bryce? Has Bryce heard from her?"

The women exchanged a quick glance and Millie immediately suspected they knew something.

"I...don't know." Kimberly averted her gaze.

"She's intentionally avoiding us," Sierra blurted out. "Bryce is almost certain she's been inside their cabin. We also know where she's been staying."

Millie almost said, 'hiding out in the lifeboats,' but bit her tongue. "Where?"

"She's been staying with another passenger. I think she said his name was Drew."

"Drew."

"Yeah. Sierra and I already called down to security to let them know," Kimberly said. "There's one more thing she said, and I'm not sure I believe it."

Chapter 18

"What did Harper say?" Millie prompted.

"She's not returning to the ship," Kimberly said.

"Because she thinks she's in trouble, which, if she is behind the vandalism and stealing not only other passengers' property but also ship's property, then she should be concerned," Millie said.

"That's part of it. She wasn't called back for a role in a show and is depressed about it," Sierra said.

"She needs help," Millie said. "And if she doesn't get back on board, who knows what will happen to her?"

"She said the guy she met, Drew, isn't getting back on either."

"If what you're saying is true, it will be on them to figure out how they'll get home," Millie warned.

"We told her that." Kimberly wrinkled her nose. "She's done stuff like this before."

"Caused a lot of problems and then left before she had to face the consequences?"

"Yep. Hopefully, she took her meds with her. Once she's off those, it's hard telling what she'll do." Kimberly told Millie they had Patterson's number and would let him know if or when they heard from Harper again.

After they left, Millie swung by the guest services desk to track down "Drew's" cabin number.

As luck would have it, there was only one "Drew" on board. His cabin was on the opposite end of the ship, several decks above Harper and Bryce's cabin. Perhaps the troubled woman wouldn't re-board, knowing she was in hot water.

Regardless, Millie was certain Patterson had a handle on the gangway and there was no way the woman could waltz back on board without being caught.

The deadline for returning to the ship came and went and Millie ran up to the lido deck to host the sailaway party. Tomorrow was the last port day before Siren of the Seas would begin making the journey home.

Limbo on the lido kicked the party off. Felix arrived and took over while Millie stood near the railing, watching as the ship drifted away from the dock. She made a quick call down to the gangway to see if all passengers had re-boarded.

The person on duty wasn't certain, but promised to have Suharto return her call. Millie placed a second call, this one to Patterson's office.

"Hello, Millie."

"Hey, Patterson. Did Harper Rothshield get back on the ship?"

"You heard."

"I ran into her friends during bingo. There was another person she was with—a man—who she claimed wasn't getting back on either."

"Drew Kane," Patterson said. "He returned to the ship. I've already chatted with him. He claims he met Harper Rothshield once and knows nothing about where she is or what she's been up to."

"Interesting," Millie murmured. "And Harper?"

"She didn't re-board via the passenger gangway."

"Meaning you suspect she may have somehow managed to get back on the ship undetected."

"It's possible. She made a point of making sure we heard she didn't plan to re-board."

"The only other way to get back on would be the crew gangway."

"We also monitored that entrance and weren't able to locate her." Patterson sighed heavily. "We'll continue to keep extra security staff making their rounds. Her family has been in contact, as well.

Apparently, Ms. Rothshield has broken up with her boyfriend. That tidbit of information is just between you and me."

"My lips are zipped," Millie said. "It could be the last straw and now she's seriously going to freak out."

"If you and the entertainment staff could keep an eye out for her, I would appreciate it."

"We'll help in any way we can." Millie promised to call an emergency staff meeting. Thanks to Andy's handy dandy scheduler app, she quickly arranged the meeting and headed downstairs to wait for whoever was available to arrive.

The backstage quickly filled, and Millie wasted no time.

"Thank you for joining me on such short notice. A passenger is showing some troubling behavior. We believe she may have destroyed some of the ship's property, including turning on the theater's auxiliary sprinklers and helped herself to a passenger's mobility scooter as well as Sharky Kiveski's scooter. We're concerned this woman might not be done, and since she appears to be most active late in the evening, I need your help."

Millie accessed the passenger roster, pulled up Harper's photo, and beamed it onto the backstage screen. "Harper Rothshield has blond or light brown hair, is roughly five feet, six inches tall, and is on the thin side."

"I think I've seen her around," Tara Daughtery said. "It was during late-night karaoke either last night or the night before."

Several other employees chimed in, claiming they may have seen the woman but, when pressed, couldn't guarantee it.

"If you see her or anyone resembling this woman, please don't confront her or give any indication she's being monitored. Contact security and advise them of her exact location," Millie said.

A staff member standing next to Millie lifted her hand. "You said she destroyed some of the ship's property. What happened?"

"We believe she used Sharky's scooter to break into the spa and then went on a rampage, destroying products and damaging expensive equipment."

A low murmur spread among the crowd.

"We're not one hundred percent certain she's behind it. At the very least, Dave Patterson would like to locate the woman and chat with her." Millie fielded several more questions and then dismissed the group.

Tara lingered, waiting for the room to clear. "I didn't want to ask in front of the others, but is there any word on Andy?"

"I spoke to him yesterday. He's certain he'll be back with us for the next voyage."

"I've been worried about him. I hope he'll be all right."

"Me too. He's in good spirits and optimistic, which is important."

"Right." Tara pressed her palms together. "All the comments from the passengers have been positive. The parade was awesome. I know a lot has been thrown at you and wanted to let you know I think you're doing a great job."

"Thanks, Tara. I have some big shoes to fill, but I'm trying."

"I've worked for several other cruise directors and have to say you and Andy are an 'A-Team.' You never miss a beat." Tara left, and Millie lingered, grateful for the ship's staff and their support. The cruise director's schedule was non-stop. Being in charge of entertaining thousands of passengers week in and week out was no small task.

But some of that credit had to go to Andy. He had trained Millie to be the best assistant cruise director she could be and when he returned, she was going to tell him exactly how much it meant to her.

She jumped into her last segment of her long workday, hustling here, running there and checking on the live entertainment.

The later the hour, the more anxious Millie became. Had Harper somehow figured out a way to sneak back on?

Finally, Millie's shift ended and it was time to go home. She made her way onto the bridge and found Nic, Donovan, Patterson, Oscar and Suharto on hand, concerned expressions etched on their faces.

"What's going on?"

"A passenger by the name of Melodee Vance has contacted the ship," Patterson said. "She was left behind in Curacao, claiming someone slipped something in her drink while she was at the beach and stole her identification including her keycard."

"How awful. We had no idea she missed the ship?"

"No. Not until she contacted us. Ms. Vance is tall, thin and blond and was befriended by a woman who is also a passenger. She's insisting this woman was the one who drugged her."

Millie's heart plummeted. "Let me guess–the person who slipped something in her drink and took her keycard was Harper Rothshield."

Chapter 19

"We believe that's what happened. Harper Rothshield stole Melodee Vance's shipboard identification. In fact, we're almost certain of it. We've located the security photo of the passenger left behind." Nic motioned to the computer monitor sitting on the conference table. "We've arranged for her to catch up with the ship tomorrow when we arrive in Bonaire."

Millie studied the woman's photo. Although it was only a headshot, there were distinct similarities between Melodee and Harper. If a large group of passengers re-boarded the ship at the same time, Harper could have slipped through, pretending to be Melodee.

"We've been in contact with Harper's companions, her boyfriend and two friends. None of them have heard from her since earlier today," Patterson said.

"I just..." Millie's voice faded.

"Just what?" Oscar prompted.

"Find it odd she's only had limited contact with her friends and boyfriend. Someone has to be helping her. I guess I get the boyfriend thing. Reading between the lines, it appears their relationship has been on the rocks for a while." Millie had another thought. "Has anyone checked to see if the lifeboat's hatches have been tampered with?"

Patterson gave a thumbs down. "Nope. I agree with you that someone is helping Harper avoid being caught. The question is, who or why?"

"What about her new 'friend' Drew? Have you talked to him again?"

"He swears he doesn't know what Harper has been up to. He let us search his cabin and I believe he's telling the truth," Patterson said.

"I suppose he has no reason to lie." Millie headed to the apartment. Perhaps if they were able to figure out what made Harper tick, they could put together a better plan of action to catch her.

After taking Scout out for a break, Millie settled in front of the computer and typed Harper's name into the search bar. Several stories popped up, one most recently about an incident at a nightclub in New York where Harper was kicked out.

The details sounded eerily similar to what had occurred on board the ship. She argued with a companion, caused a scene, destroyed property and was escorted out. Not long after, Harper checked into the rehab, which, judging by the timeline, was the one she was in when she decided she'd had enough, checked out early and boarded the ship.

Along with the story was a short clip, a scene from when she was on the reality show. Millie's scalp tingled as she read the series title, "The Great Evade." A blurb followed the title. "Would you be willing to elude detection for a shot at winning a hundred grand? Follow along with our contestants as they use their wits to be the last person standing in the town of Dodge City."

The premise of the show was for the contestants to avoid being caught. Meanwhile, the locals were on the lookout for them, winning points and prizes for each contestant they located.

Harper made it to the final three and was finally spotted by a teenager who used a nighttime heat detection device to track her down.

"She thinks this is all a game," Millie whispered. "This unstable passenger has turned our cruise ship into her own reality game."

Millie read the first story a second time, this one about her altercation at the bar. A small quote at the bottom sounded so much of what Harper had said to her, basically refusing to accept any responsibility. She also made a point of saying she had a new show "in the works," something new and fresh and never done before.

“Bryce Bridges, my manager, is finalizing the details. We plan to make an announcement soon,” Harper was quoted as saying.

The apartment door opened, and Nic appeared. “Still hard at work?”

“I’m hard at work trying to figure out what makes Harper Rothshield tick.” Millie filled Nic in on her discovery.

“She was in a reality show where the goal was to avoid being found,” Nic said.

“Yes. Bryce Bridges, her boyfriend, is also her manager.”

“Which means he knows a lot more about where she is and what she’s doing than he’s letting on,” Nic said.

“That would be my guess.” Millie shifted. “Think about it. They’re working together to help her avoid being caught. What if we, meaning Siren of the Seas, is her new reality show? How much exposure would she get if she caused chaos and took all of what she'd done back to the producers? If she could sell them on a new series, she's back in the spotlight and has figured out a way to jumpstart her career."

"It seems a little out there, but stranger things have happened."

"Exactly. If the woman is off her meds, meanwhile trying to remain relevant, who knows what she's capable of?" Millie slid out of the chair and wandered to the balcony. Off in the distance, she could see the twinkling lights of Bonaire, their last port stop, before heading home.

If Harper Rothshield was trying to "make a splash" and capture headline news, she would have to ramp up her antics. She remembered the missing flares and mentioned them to Nic.

"I'm hoping she doesn't resort to using them. It would create a panic. The security staff has been notified some are missing, but again, we can't be everywhere all the time. It doesn't help if Rothshield is an expert at avoiding detection."

"We need to come up with a plan to lure her out."

"I agree, but how?"

"I'm not sure. I'll have to think about it."

Nic gazed out into the starry night, and Millie could tell something was troubling him.

"Is everything all right?"

"Huh?"

Millie slipped in next to him. "Is everything all right? You look like you have the weight of the world sitting on your shoulders."

Nic smiled sadly. "I spoke to Andy earlier."

Their eyes met, and her husband looked away.

"He has news."

"A tentative diagnosis," Nic said. "It doesn't look good."

"Nic." Millie swallowed hard, sudden tears blurring her vision.

"It's not for certain, and I promised Andy I wouldn't tell anyone. They believe they know what's wrong with him, but have one more test to run before giving a final diagnosis."

"He has to be all right," she whispered.

"I know." Nic pulled her into his arms. "I shouldn't have said anything."

"We need to pray."

Nic and Millie bowed their heads and held hands.

"Dear God, please help Andy. Please help the doctors figure out what's wrong and fix him," Millie prayed. Unable to go on, she squeezed Nic's hand.

"We pray for healing in his body and that you give him and Cat peace during the process."

"Amen," the couple echoed in unison.

"Let's not worry until we have the final word," Nic cautioned.

"Which is easier said than done."

Nic locked up and Millie followed him upstairs to get ready for bed. After finishing, she slipped beneath the covers and prayed for Andy again, for peace and wisdom for the doctors. Finally, she fell asleep. It was a light, restless sleep and every time she woke, her first thought was about Andy and Cat. Harper Rothshield and the woman's next move were a close second.

Obviously, the troublesome passenger had to know the person whose identity she stole would contact the ship. They would easily put two and two together, figuring out Harper had sneaked her way back on board.

She couldn't shake the feeling the woman wasn't acting alone. Someone had to be helping her, but who? Her boyfriend? Her friends? "Drew," her new acquaintance?

The only solution was to outsmart the woman and come up with a plan to get her to come to them.

*****

Beep. Beep. Beep. Millie bolted upright. Her eyes flew to the clock.

Nic groaned as he threw the covers back. "Is it time already?"

"Unfortunately." Millie let Nic get ready first, knowing he would need to be on the bridge early to guide the cruise ship into port.

She lingered a little longer, checking her email and then going over the stories about Harper Rothshield a second time. The woman was desperate for attention. It didn't matter whether it was good or bad as long as she got it.

There was no doubt in Millie's mind she wasn't done causing trouble. If anything, she was going to ramp it up to a level that drew even greater attention. The flares were an enormous concern.

She thought about the tracking tag Sharky had found stuck to his scooter's battery cover. Obviously, it belonged to Harper. What had she planned to do with it?

Millie grabbed a scratchpad and pen and jotted down what she knew about the woman.

Mental instability. On medication.

Checked out of rehab.

Relationship issues with (ex) boyfriend.

Previous displays of conflict and confrontation.

Able to avoid detection.

Seeking the spotlight by whatever means possible.

Millie started a second list, this one of what Harper had done since boarding Siren of the Seas:

Caused scene in the nightclub. Fought with boyfriend and bartender.

Confronted Millie, and accused her of calling her a liar. Told her she would be sorry.

Stole passenger's scooter and drove it into the pool.

Hiding out in one of the lifeboats.

Sneaked into the parade. Left costume and keys for staff to find.

Turned sprinklers on in theater.

Stole Sharky's scooter and broke into the spa, destroying product and damaging his scooter.

Stole some of the ship's emergency flares?

Exited ship. Stole other pax identification to get back on.

Where is she now?

Millie underlined the last bullet point. Where was Harper, and what was her next move? That was the million dollar question.

She folded the notes and tucked them into her pocket before heading to Andy's office for the early morning staff meeting. Millie filled them in on her suspicions that Harper was still somewhere on the ship and asked them to keep an eye out for her before dismissing the group.

Danielle waited for the room to clear. "She's still at it."

Millie told Danielle what she'd discovered, about the details of the reality television show season where her main goal was to perform certain tasks while not getting caught.

"I told you I remember watching parts of it but didn't finish. Did she win?" Danielle asked.

"No, but she made it to the top three. She was also quoted as saying she was working on a new project. As far as I know, the emergency flares are still missing. I'm almost certain she has them and, to top it all off, someone is helping her remain undetected," Millie said.

"The boyfriend or one of her friends?"

"Or Drew, the man she met." Millie removed the notes from her pocket. "I'm having serious doubts we'll be able to locate her. We need to figure out a way to lure her to us."

"You're clever, Millie. I'm sure you'll think of something," Danielle said.

Kevin, one of the ship's dancers, appeared in the doorway. "Knock. Knock."

Millie motioned him inside.

"I can come back later if you're busy."

"No. We're done."

"I wanted to let you know you're doing a great job. I'm sure Andy would be proud of you."

"Thank you. I'm trying my best," Millie said. "All of you make my job easier, pitching in to do whatever is needed."

"I was wondering if I might take another look at the picture of the passenger in hiding."

"Of course." Millie pulled up Harper's shipboard photo.

Kevin grew quiet as he studied it. "That's her."

Millie's heart skipped a beat. "You've seen this woman?"

"I have. She took part in the escape room adventure yesterday."

"What time was that?" Millie began flipping through the previous day's schedule.

"It was early evening. The reason I remember her was because she was picky about which team she wanted to be on. It was almost as if she was interviewing them."

"How?" Millie asked.

"Wanting to know if they'd ever done an escape room before. If they were on the winning or losing team, stuff like that," Kevin said.

"Let me guess...she was part of the winning team," Millie said.

"She was. The others in her group were getting annoyed with her. She kind of took over and ran the show."

“Sounds about right.”

“I heard you talking to Danielle about how you wished there was a way you could draw her out into the open,” Kevin said. “I think I have an idea.”

Chapter 20

"If the woman is the one you're looking for, she wanted to know if I was hosting another escape room event," Kevin said. "I told her there was one more this evening and I'm almost positive she plans to attend."

Millie clapped her hands. "This is the best news I've had all week."

"You know her better than I do. Maybe you should host it instead of me."

Millie quickly shot down the idea. "She doesn't like me."

Danielle tapped her arm. "You said you thought she had help, someone who was making sure she wasn't found or caught."

"I do."

"Which means before we can set a trap to catch her, we need to lay the groundwork and chat with her traveling companions," Danielle said. "We want them to think we believe Harper got off the ship yesterday and never got back on."

"Good point."

"If Patterson and his men continue with their patrols and extra searches, they're going to know we suspect she's still on board."

"I'm following you," Millie said. "So you think we should convince Patterson to pull back on the hunt for Harper? She'll let her guard down and..."

"Bam." Danielle smacked her palms together. "We trap her in the escape room."

"Wouldn't that be the perfect justice?" Millie's excitement quickly faded. "How in the world are we going to get Patterson to go along with it?"

"Patterson likes to cut deals. Cut a deal with him."

In theory, Danielle's idea to convince Patterson to halt searching for the troublesome passenger made the most sense, but the head of the security department was a cut-and-dried by-the-book person. Persuading him to go along with the idea was going to be tricky.

Before Millie could even think about tracking him down, she needed to head to the gangway to see passengers off.

Long lines snaked along the corridor and up the side stairs. Millie made her way to the spot she and Andy had stood side by side so many times, chatting during the quiet moments, about life on the high seas, about Andy's plans and his future with Cat.

His larger-than-life personality was sorely missed and she could feel herself getting teary-eyed at the thought of something being seriously wrong with him. He wasn't just her boss; he was her friend, her confidante, her mentor. Millie couldn't love Andy Walker any more than if he was her very own flesh and blood.

Several of the "regulars" stopped to chat, noting his absence and asking about him. Each time, she explained he was on leave but would be returning soon.

The crowds exiting the ship remained steady for longer than normal. Finally, there was a lull, and Millie darted over to the gangway. "Is it me or have a lot of the passengers gotten off?"

"We have been very busy," Suharto said. "It is typically the case for the last port day. I think passengers decide they would like to put their feet on dry land before we make the long journey back to port."

Because the ABC Islands were among the most southern port stops, the journey back to Florida stretched out for two, and sometimes even three, long days.

Millie bounced on the tips of her toes, peering over the edge of Suharto's counter. "How many have gotten off?"

Suharto rattled off a large number. "Eighty percent of the passengers have exited the ship."

"Woo-hoo." Millie let out a whoop. "The crew has the ship to themselves."

"It would appear so." Suharto smiled. "Have you heard from Andy?"

"I spoke to him the other day. He's in good spirits, but ready to get back."

"He is a very busy man. He likes to go, go, go. I imagine the doctors are having a hard time keeping him down."

"I'm sure they are." Millie told Suharto she would return around boarding time and headed upstairs to the Sky Chapel.

She stepped inside and a faint light radiated from the sanctuary's podium. Millie eased the door shut behind her and tiptoed down the center aisle. As she drew closer, she could see light shining from beneath Pastor Evans' office door and the sound of soft music playing.

A sense of peace enveloped Millie as she eased onto the empty pew and stared at the cross. She bowed her head and closed her eyes, praying fervently for her friend.

Millie swiped at the lone tear that trickled down her cheek. She lifted her head, watching as Pastor Evans made his way toward her. "I thought I heard someone."

"I had a few minutes and wanted to have a quiet word with God."

The pastor took a step back. "Don't let me intrude."

"I've finished." Millie slowly stood. "This is my sanctuary away from the crazy. I needed to come here to catch my breath."

"I completely understand and have done the same many times." Pastor Evans folded his arms. "How is Andy?"

"Hanging in there. I'm worried," Millie confessed.

"I'm sure you are. A lot of people are praying for him."

The two made small talk, and Millie could feel her heart lighten. God would take care of Andy—and Cat. It was up to her to trust and believe.

*****

Millie's morning hours dragged and the attendance of almost every event was low. Near noon, she swung by the galley, grabbed a RTG sack lunch and ran downstairs to the security office.

Patterson wasn't around, so Millie retraced her steps, juggling her cell phone in one hand as she tapped out a message to him. She rounded the corner, nearly colliding with the head of security.

"Hasn't anyone ever told you it's a bad idea to text and walk?"

"Better than texting and driving." Millie motioned to the tray of food he was carrying and held up her sack lunch. "Care to join me for a bite to eat?"

"Sure. Let's head to the dining room. I was going to eat in my office, but sometimes it's nice to have a change of scenery."

It was a fast trek to the crewmembers' dining area and, like the passenger areas, there were very few people inside, making it easy to find an empty table and a quiet corner.

"You were hunting me down for a reason," Patterson guessed as soon as they sat.

"I am. It's about Harper Rothshield. You still believe she's on board the ship."

"I do. I met with Melodee Vance. She confirmed Harper was the woman who approached her at the beach, bought her a drink and drugged her."

“How did she do that exactly?” Millie smeared a thick layer of mustard on her BLT club sandwich and took a big bite.

“The two met the first day while boarding. Melodee mentioned how she’d visited the island before and planned to head to one of her favorite beaches in Curacao. Harper showed up while she was there. They hung out. Harper offered to buy them drinks. Next thing Melodee knew, she was passed out in her lounge chair and Harper was long gone.”

“And so was Melodee’s ship card and identification.”

“Correct. It appears Harper had planned the ‘chance encounter’ with the goal of exiting the ship and re-boarding using Melodee’s identification.”

“The woman is diabolically clever,” Millie said. “At some level, you have to admire her resourcefulness.”

"While simultaneously wanting to strangle her," Patterson joked.

"I take it you haven't had any luck locating her?"

"Nope."

"I think we're going about it all wrong," Millie said. "We need to work smarter, not harder."

"And how do you propose we do that?" Patterson asked.

"By luring her to us."

"I take it you have an idea."

Millie filled him in on her conversation with Kevin and how they suspected Harper had taken part in the escape room activity. "She seemed very interested in the one he's hosting later this evening. I was thinking of maybe disguising myself. I could play along with the others, wait for the opportune moment, and catch her."

"It could be dangerous," Patterson warned.

"Not if we plan it right," Millie argued. "We'll need to get the other passengers away from her first, corner her in the escape room, and then...Voila! You have Harper, beating her at her own game."

"I like the idea. It might work."

"With one caveat."

"Caveat?" Patterson's eyes narrowed.

"That you call off your search for her." Millie hurried on. "You haven't been able to get her. If she thinks you believe she left the ship, she might let her guard down."

"How do we do that? Announce it over the loudspeaker?"

"You said yourself you think someone is helping her, so all we have to do is spread the word to the people most likely to be helping and they inadvertently relay the message."

"Hmmm." Patterson made an unhappy sound.

"I know it goes against everything you've been trained, but if we're going to get her and plan to do it on our terms, we need to make sure those terms are leaning in our favor," Millie said.

"I suppose it won't hurt. Besides, my guys could use a break. They've been working nonstop trying to track her down."

"See?" Millie dusted her hands. "It's a win-win. They get a break. Meanwhile, we put the pieces in place to stop the woman once and for all."

"What if you set the trap in the escape room and it doesn't work—or worse, backfires?"

"Then you go back to all hands on deck and search every nook and cranny of the ship," Millie said.

She could see Patterson weighing her argument. "I'm willing to try it, but only because there's a good chance she still has access to the missing flares. She's like a ticking time bomb and right now, all we're doing is trying to prepare ourselves for when she goes off."

"All the better reason to do it our way instead of letting her continue this cat and mouse game. She thrives on this sort of thing. It's a power trip and gives her some sort of sick thrill knowing she has the ship's crewmembers and officers, including you, in an uproar."

"You have my approval. As soon as I finish eating, I'll pull everyone back and return them to their regular schedules. Maybe even Oscar can get some rest." Patterson wagged his finger. "But only until tomorrow. If we can't nab her today, we go back to Plan A."

Millie extended her hand. "It's a deal."

Patterson grudgingly shook it. "And one more thing. I want in on the sting."

"I figured you would. This is our chance. It will be a one and done so we need to make sure the plan is foolproof; the other participants are safe and Harper's trapped with no escape from the escape room."

Chapter 21

"You designed all of this yourself?" Millie stepped inside what had once been one of the ship's conference rooms, also known as the "flex space." The space had housed Andy's fall-themed maze, an overflow for the craft classes, and was now Kevin's brainchild, an escape room.

"Welcome to 'Cruise, Clues and Crimes.' This is a sixty-minute escape room where you'll need to solve puzzles, uncover clues and maybe even crack codes to find your way out."

Patterson elbowed Millie. "You're a super sleuth. I'm surprised this wasn't your idea."

"I have to admit, I love it and am intrigued. I'm actually looking forward to playing along." Millie rubbed her hands together. "Pretend we're participants and show us how it all works."

"I would love to." Kevin pressed a button. A projector lowered from the ceiling and a video began playing on the wall's whiteboard.

Soft concerto piano echoed in the background. Kevin appeared, sporting a plaid Sherlock Holmes deerstalker cap and a gray tweed overcoat with a tan pipe casually clenched between his teeth. He removed the pipe and cleared his throat as he addressed the camera.

"Hello, and welcome to Siren of the Seas' Cruise, Clues and Crimes adventure. I'm Kevin, your host." He leaned in and lowered his voice. "We have reason to believe Dave Patterson, the head of the ship's security department, is involved in an art theft ring."

"What?" Patterson roared. "You made me a part of your crime?"

Danielle clamped a hand over her mouth and snorted through her nose. "This is great."

"Great?"

Kevin pressed the pause button. "It's all in good fun. Donovan Sweeney is the suspect in the other escape game."

"I love it." Millie burst out laughing. "I couldn't have planned it better myself. Let's keep watching."

Patterson shot daggers at them and sullenly eyed the screen.

Kevin hit the play button. "The ship's officers and crew view Patterson as a straight shooter, who goes by the book, but I suspect he's become caught up in making some side cash by smuggling valuable art from the ship. A recent audit revealed two pieces in particular have gone missing. So far, we've been able to ascertain Patterson personally oversaw the transport of both."

The missing pieces appeared on the screen and then Kevin reappeared. "We believe both are located in the room behind me." Kevin glanced at his watch. "Patterson is attending a meeting at this very minute. According to my sources, we have precisely sixty minutes to find the paintings before he returns to his office."

"You'll also need to be aware Patterson's team is patrolling the ship. We're uncertain about their level of involvement, but if they are, these men could quite possibly be his partners."

Oscar's mugshot appeared, along with Suharto.

Millie clutched her gut. "This is so awesome. Oh my gosh. I love it."

Kevin continued speaking. "There is one more person to watch out for. We suspect he may also be involved."

Sharky, perched atop his scooter and Fin in the basket, appeared grinning from ear-to-ear.

"Sharky, our maintenance supervisor, and his sidekick cat, Fin."

Tears rolled down Millie's cheeks while Patterson shot her an annoyed look.

"Does Sharky know he's a part of your escape game?"

"Yeah. It was his idea to be included. He wanted to be a villain."

"I suppose I shouldn't be surprised." Patterson rolled his eyes.

"Here's your mission," Kevin said in a low voice. "Figure out how to sneak into Patterson's office, track down these two pieces of artwork, and get out before he returns."

He leaned in, staring straight into the camera. "You look like an intelligent bunch. This should be an easy assignment. Get in, locate the stolen art and get out. A word of warning...if Patterson finds you inside." Kevin made a slicing motion across his neck. "I would hate to see what happens. If you want to back out, now's your chance."

There was a long pause. "Are you up to the challenge?" Kevin lifted the pipe in a snappy salute and winked. "I pegged you for daring risk-takers and I see I wasn't wrong. I'll be keeping an eye on you from right here in the storage room. Stay safe, work together, and we'll see you back here in an hour or less. The clock is ticking. Go!"

The video abruptly ended, and Millie applauded. "Bravo. It looks like a blast."

"Thanks," Kevin beamed. "Andy and I worked hard on this. The passengers seem to love it."

"I think we should do it," Millie said.

"I..."

"C'mon, Patterson. It will be fun."

"I'm in," Danielle said. "I think it'll be great."

"It might be helpful for you to know exactly how the escape room works so you can figure out the precise moment you want to nab Rothshield," Kevin said.

"How many people will take part?"

"The max amount is eight. Any more than that and everyone is tripping all over each other. So, are you going to give it a go?"

Patterson rubbed his chin. "All right. Let's do it." He reluctantly followed Millie and Danielle into the escape room, aka his office. "This doesn't even look like my office," he grumbled.

"We had to alter the appearance, so there was room for clues." Kevin held the door. "I'll monitor the entire event. When the actual group arrives, I'll be keeping an eye on them from outside."

"What types of clues are we searching for?" Danielle asked.

"Look for patterns or connections. It could be something as simple as a hidden key. Clues and puzzle pieces are hidden all over inside this room and each one helps you complete your mission," Kevin said. "Which is to figure out where Patterson is keeping the artwork. One more suggestion: when you locate a clue, start piling them up so the others can see what you have."

Kevin wished them luck and pulled the door shut behind him.

Millie noticed a large black clock. "We're down to fifty-nine minutes and ten seconds."

The trio split up, and Millie began tapping the walls. Danielle dropped to her knees and studied the floor while Patterson began searching the desk. "You two should be experts at this, considering how many times you've stuck your nose in where it doesn't belong and rifled through personal property without permission."

"And helped solve a mystery or two," Millie pointed out. "We need to come up with a plan, how we're going to separate Harper from the others in the group."

"I have a better idea," Patterson said. "This is a sting, to catch her."

"Correct."

"We bring other crewmembers in as participants."

Danielle arched a brow. "That's a great idea. She arrives thinking she's playing the escape game with other passengers. Meanwhile, she's surrounded by the ship's staff."

"My plan is to play a little old lady," Millie said. "There are some old costumes in the storage closet. I have one in mind that will work perfectly."

"I was thinking of asking Annette to join you. She has a skill set that would be useful. I doubt Harper has met her. We'll also need some muscle." Patterson lifted the desk lamp and twisted the base. "I found one. It says, 'Finding clues is a walk in the park.'"

"A walk in the park." Millie's eyes fell on the shoe tray near the door. "Walk as in feet as in shoes."

Danielle, still on all fours, scampered to the tray and flipped it over, revealing a note taped to the bottom. "Bingo. Good job, Patterson."

"Back to Harper," Patterson said. "We could have you in disguise, Danielle in disguise, Annette in regular clothes."

"Brody is a big guy, but he's also all over this ship."

"And his voice is easily recognizable," Millie said. "You could lurk in the background, watching from the wings and then pounce on her as soon as she exits the escape room after it's over."

"What about Felix?" Millie suggested.

"I'm sure she would recognize him," Patterson said.

"He could be our group guide. She probably wouldn't think anything of it." Millie warmed to the idea. "Kevin could pitch it that Felix is taking over as the escape room guide and will be participating to see how it runs."

"It's...an option." Patterson ran his hand along the back of the chair and down the side. He felt along the inside of the frame and pulled out a folded sheet of paper with an attached pen. "What do we have here?"

Millie darted to his side. "Invisible ink and a pen."

"It's all yours."

"Sweet." Millie laid it flat on the desk and began scribbling. "You're getting hotter."

"That's the clue?" Danielle sprang to her feet. "You're getting hotter?"

"False leads. False clues. I suppose it's all part of the game and another way for the clock to keep ticking." With renewed determination, Danielle and Millie, along with Patterson's half-hearted attempt, found the paintings and the key to unlock the escape room door.

Kevin stood waiting on the other side and applauded. "You made it under the wire. Only about thirty percent are able to track down all of the clues and find their way out."

Patterson thumbed his finger at Danielle and Millie. "We're dealing with a couple professionals here."

"So?" Kevin took the key from Danielle. "Do you think you can make it work?"

"Is this the only way out?"

"It is," Kevin said.

Patterson spun in a slow circle. "I do believe it could work," he said. "Whether Harper Rothshield shows is another story."

Chapter 22

"I think she'll show." Millie consulted her watch, noting the escape game, Cruise, Clues and Crimes, was starting soon. She grabbed a compact from her purse and flipped it open, critically eyeing her disguise.

"You look great." Danielle scrunched the front of her turquoise ball cap with the glittery *One Happy Island, Aruba* emblazoned on the front. "How did I do on mine?"

"You'll blend right in." Millie tapped Annette's shoulder. "I was thinking...Harper doesn't have any unique features, no scars or moles to look for."

"Which could easily be covered by makeup," Annette pointed out. "She can't change her height or weight, so we'll have to be mindful of the participants who fit her criteria—tall and thin."

Felix sashayed over. "You all look fabulous," he gushed. "Who has Patterson's backup plan?"

"He does," Millie said. "I don't think we're going to need it. Harper's going to show. We wait until the very end of the escape room game and while the attendees are exiting the area, we whisk her off in the other direction, where Patterson is waiting to apprehend her."

Kevin arrived, along with Patterson and Oscar.

"I spoke with Kimberly, Sierra and Bryce," Patterson said.

"And told them you and the security team believed Harper never returned to the ship," Annette said.

"Correct. I asked them to let me know if they received any communication from her and that we would be reporting her missing to the local authorities. I even had them fill out the missing persons' paperwork." Patterson pulled a pack of papers from his pocket and handed them to Kevin.

"What are these?"

"Plan B. Pass these out to the participants at the end."

Kevin studied the sheets. "These are casino vouchers."

"Trackable casino vouchers. As soon as the player tries to redeem them, the casino's players club is notified of what machine. If Harper shows up, she'll get one. The bait is enticing enough that I'm hoping everyone will redeem them."

Kevin's watch app chimed. "It's showtime!"

Millie, Annette, and Danielle circled around, exiting via the crew corridor and then back through the main entrance. A group had already gathered and Kevin stood nearby greeting them.

Millie checked in under her fake name. Danielle and Annette weren't far behind.

Kevin passed out pads of paper and a brief instruction sheet, and while Millie skimmed the list, she furtively studied the group.

None of the attendees even remotely resembled Harper Rothshield. She caught Danielle's eye and got the same impression that she had not located the woman, either.

"I think everyone is here." Kevin nudged Felix forward. "Felix will be taking over the escape room events and is joining you as a participant."

Felix gave a cheery wave. "I love a good mystery."

Kevin went over the nuts and bolts of the game and then played the video Millie and the others had watched earlier. She smiled again when Patterson's picture popped up, followed by Oscar, Suharto, and Sharky.

"The object of the game is to search the head of security's office for the two valuable paintings in question," Kevin said. "Here's what they look like."

Millie was surprised to see two entirely different paintings than the ones she and the others had found, suspecting Kevin had “tweaked” the event.

The video ended. Kevin passed out the initial clues and Millie pulled him aside. “You switched things around.”

“Of course.” Kevin winked at her. “It wouldn’t be much fun, considering you already had the clues and could figure it out.”

Felix led the others into the room while Millie lingered. “Have you seen her?”

“No. Maybe she got spooked.” Kevin peered over Millie’s shoulder. “The skinny guy that came in last was giving me a weird vibe. Maybe she’s in disguise too.”

“Wouldn’t that be something?”

“We still have Patterson’s backup plan.” Kevin patted his pocket. “Good luck.”

"Thanks. We're going to need it." Millie slipped into the back of the room, watching as Felix took charge of the group, basically repeating what Kevin had already said.

They split up, and Millie began searching the walls, running a light hand across the wallpaper until she found a groove. It was a small latch. She gently tugged on it, revealing a scrolled paper. "I found something."

The others gathered around as she unrolled the clue. The tall gentlemen who had hit Millie's radar from the beginning drew closer and she caught a whiff of perfume. Her heart skipped a beat as the "man" leaned in even closer. "We should check the light's base for a clue which illuminates."

The others faded away, including the man. He was strangely quiet, not speaking, and Millie thought she might know the reason.

Annette caught her eye and with the slightest nod of her head, motioned to the tall stranger, Heath.

Millie pretended to continue searching, and the more she watched, the more certain she was that "he" was wearing a disguise. A snippet of blond hair became clearly visible as Heath knelt next to the rug and began searching the floor beneath it.

Millie reached for her cell phone, intending to send Patterson a text, and then remembered cell phones weren't allowed.

The minutes ticked by. At the forty-nine-minute mark, at least according to the loud tick-tock of the wall clock, the group tracked down the last clue and located both paintings along with the key to unlock the door.

Kevin stood on the other side, clapping loudly and congratulating the group on making it through. "We have some very clever sleuths in this group. I believe you may have set a record for the shortest amount of time to recover the artwork and open the door." He began passing out the vouchers. "These vouchers are good for twenty-five dollars in free play at Winning Streak Casino. The only catch is they must be used by midnight tonight."

"Midnight tonight?" a woman griped. "What if I don't want to use it before then?"

"It turns into a pumpkin," Kevin joked.

"Do you have anything else?" a man asked.

"I do." Kevin reached into the small brown box next to him and held up a ship on a stick. "I also have a ship on a stick."

"Thanks, but no thanks."

"I'm sorry you're not happy with the prizes," Kevin apologized. "Unfortunately, I ran out of specialty shop coffee coupons."

No one swapped their casino voucher for a ship on a stick, and Felix led them down the hall. Millie, Annette, and Danielle hung back, waiting for the area to clear.

"Well?" Kevin asked. "Did you figure out which one was Harper?"

"I think it was the tall guy wearing women's perfume," Millie said.

"I smelled it too," Danielle said. "Ten bucks says it was Harper in disguise."

Heavy footsteps echoed, and Patterson appeared. "I heard voices. Is the escape room ending soon?"

"It's over. We had a super snoopy bunch. They made it out in record time," Kevin said.

"You mean they're already gone? Harper got away?"

"Harper may or may not have been in the group," Danielle said. "If she was, she was wearing a disguise."

"We'll have to go with backup Plan B. They all took the casino vouchers." Millie waved her voucher in the air.

"Great." Patterson briefly closed his eyes. "I'll have to station someone near the casino for the duration of the cruise."

A sly smile spread across Kevin's face. "Only until midnight tonight."

"Kevin told everyone they had to use the vouchers by midnight tonight," Annette said.

"You did?" Patterson gave him a hearty whack on the back. "That's brilliant."

Millie faked Andy's British accent. "Or as Andy would say...bloody brilliant."

Danielle tapped the top of her watch. "If Harper was in the crowd, assuming she'll want to use her casino voucher, you have only a few hours to try and catch her."

Millie did a mental calculation. "There were only four other players besides us. Looking back, I'm almost certain she was dressed like a man. See for yourself."

She showed the others the photo she'd secretly snapped of the thin man and even managed to catch the wisp of blond hair sticking out. "Do you see the blond hair? He / she was wearing a wig."

Patterson handed the phone back. "The only problem is, we can't start harassing innocent passengers. I'll have to figure out a plan to stop them to chat."

"We're already in disguise and no one in the group will think twice if they see us down there using these." Danielle waved her voucher in the air. "I say we all head to the casino and spend a couple hours waiting for the action."

"The more people around, the better our chance of nailing Harper." Patterson tapped Millie's shoulder. "If you can get someone to cover for you for a couple hours, I wouldn't mind having you in place to keep an eye out."

"I'm game to see it through. This woman has been nothing but a thorn in our sides since the very first night. The sooner we can take her down, the better."

Chapter 23

It took a few phone calls and some juggling for Millie to get her shift, along with Danielle's, covered. Amit assured Annette he could handle the galley for the rest of the evening now that the first and second seating dinners had ended.

Millie was the first to arrive at the casino, a place she rarely visited. It reminded her of Diamond Dan, the Twilight Travel singles' group host and past passenger, who Millie suspected had killed his girlfriend.

Over the years, she'd been instrumental in nabbing a few bad guys, which meant she'd amassed more than her share of enemies.

Millie thought about Cat's ex-husband, Jay, who had kidnapped her. The poor woman had been traumatized and spent time in counseling because of it.

The casino was sometimes a hotbed of trouble. Drinking and parting with hard-earned cash was a losing combination and Siren of the Seas always kept at least one security guard on duty to keep an eye out for potential problems.

She wandered up and down the rows, mesmerized by the flashing lights and ringing machines, but none struck her as appearing lucky.

Finally, she chose one based on its central location, close to the tables and midway between the slot machines. The cashier was directly ahead, with exits on either side.

"Hey." Danielle tapped Millie on the shoulder and sank down onto the seat next to her. "How's it going?"

"I haven't seen anyone even remotely resembling Harper. What if we're way off track?"

"You smelled perfume on the man and saw the wig."

"It could be a woman who likes to dress like a man." Millie's eyes scanned the area. "There's a chance he or she doesn't even show."

"Twenty-five bucks is twenty-five bucks." Danielle inserted her voucher in the machine. "What is this?"

"A penny machine." Millie tapped the penny symbol in the lower right corner of the screen.

"Sweet. It's going to take me a long time to spend twenty-five bucks a penny at a pop." Danielle's excitement quickly faded. "Crud. With a fifty-cent minimum bet."

Millie laughed. "They don't call them one-armed bandits for nothing."

Danielle tapped the play button. "I was in Vegas once."

"Sin City. You don't strike me as the gambling type."

"I was working undercover to bust up a drug ring. We weren't even close to the strip. There are some rough areas in Vegas."

"Which are found anywhere."

"I suppose." Danielle pressed the button again. "My money won't last long at this rate. I've already spent a buck. How are you doing?"

"Good. I haven't played yet," Millie said. "Maybe I'll hang onto my money and cash it in at the end of the night."

"Psst."

Millie craned her neck, peering between machines, and found Annette on the other side. "Any sign of our target?"

"Not yet," Millie said. "The night is still young."

A security guard strolled past. He gave Millie a second glance but didn't stop.

Danielle spent another dollar and then left, claiming she wanted to try another machine, this one near the door.

Millie slid down one, stuck her voucher in the machine Danielle had vacated and hit the “bet one” button. *Ding...ding...ding*. The lights flashed, and she stared at the screen.

“You won.” The woman two machines down gave her a thumbs up.

“What did I win?”

She popped out of her seat and hurried over. “That was a nice one. Two hundred and fifty.”

Millie’s jaw dropped. “Dollars?”

“Yes.” The woman tapped the flashing number on the screen. “It’s right there. You must’ve found a hot machine.”

Millie promptly hit the “cash out” button and tucked the winning ticket in her front pocket.

The woman stared in disbelief. "You're not doing a backup spin?"

"No. It was beginner's luck and I'm not willing to test it again."

"Do you mind if I play your machine?"

"Be my guest."

The woman promptly cashed out and plopped down on Millie's winning machine. "Wish me luck."

"Good luck." Millie circled the floor, searching for Harper or the skinny man. She found Danielle on an end machine. "How are you doing?"

"Okay. I won my money back. I'm at twenty-five bucks again. How about you?"

Millie grinned as she flashed her winning ticket.

Danielle's eyes grew round as saucers. "You won two hundred and fifty bucks?"

"On the machine you were playing."

"What are you going to do with it?"

"Cash it in and walk around." Millie's eyes scanned the casino floor. "Have you seen anyone interesting?"

"Nope. Annette went to the other side. This whole thing might be a bust except for you winning some ka-ching."

"Entirely by accident." Millie grew bored with the lights and sounds, and as the hours wore on, the casino became crowded. Finally, she settled on a machine near the entrance. Her cell phone vibrated. It was a text from Nic. *How's your evening going?*

Good. I'm in the casino.

Casino? he texted back.

We're trying to catch Harper Rothshield.

By playing slots?

It's a long story.

I can only imagine, Nic replied. *Be careful. Don't spend all your money.*

Millie took a picture of her winnings and sent it to him. *I'm bringing this home.*

You're a lucky lady. Have fun and stay safe.

Eleven fifteen came and went and the crowds started to thin again. She felt a tap on her shoulder and turned to find Annette standing behind her. "I'm heading up to the galley. I want to help Amit finish the last of the cleaning so he can clock out and go home."

"I'm sorry. It seems we've wasted our time."

"At least we tried." Annette stifled a yawn. "This isn't my jam. I hate losing money."

"You spent your money?"

"Spent it. Won it back. I'm quitting while I'm ahead."

"Thanks for trying to help," Millie said.

"You're welcome. It's not over. She could still show." Annette promised to catch up with her the next day, and Millie watched as she cashed in her ticket. She began making her way to the exit when a familiar figure strolled inside, head held high as if she didn't have a care in the world.

Harper looked directly at Millie, and there was no sign she recognized her. Annette saw her at the precise same moment. She did an about-face and began trailing behind.

Millie sent a quick text to Patterson. *Harper is here.*

The woman nonchalantly took a seat at a video poker machine and stuck her voucher in the slot.

A flurry of movement ensued as the ship's security staff appeared. They came at her from all directions and quickly surrounded the bank of machines.

Harper scrambled to her feet. The guards, anticipating her move, blocked her in. Seconds later, Patterson strode into the casino and straight over to their troublesome passenger. He leaned in and said something in her ear.

A look of defeat crossed Harper's face. Her shoulders slumped and, much to Millie's surprise, she didn't put up a fight as the guards escorted her from the casino.

Millie slowly removed her wig and blocked Harper's path. "Harper Rothshield. It's so nice to see you again."

Harper's eyes narrowed, and she mumbled something unpleasant under her breath.

"Let's go." Patterson continued making his way out of the casino while passengers stared.

"The bust was a little anti-climactic," Annette said after they were gone.

"No kidding. Maybe she was tired."

"Tired of hiding. Worn out from destroying personal property," Annette said.

"She left her backpack." Millie ran over and picked it up. She carried it back to where Annette and now Danielle stood waiting. "I saw her set this on the floor next to her."

"I wonder what's in Harper's bag of tricks."

"There's only one way to find out." Millie unzipped the backpack, reached inside and pulled out a flare. "The ticking timebomb, aka Harper Rothshield, was getting ready to explode."

Chapter 24

Millie leaned her elbows on the railing, watching as Harper Rothshield and her enabler boyfriend, along with Sierra and Bryce's sister Kimberly, escorted by a small army of security guards made their way down the glass ramp enclosure toward a trio of cop cars.

"That was one crazy cruise."

She twisted around to find Danielle standing behind her. "No kidding. That woman is seriously unbalanced with her boyfriend on the sideline, egging her on, no less. It's a good thing the cruise wasn't any longer. I can't imagine how much more damage she could've done."

"But we found her safe and sound, and now hopefully she'll find the strength to escape her toxic relationship," Danielle said.

"I stopped by Patterson's office a little while ago. He's tallying the damages."

"Destroying a passenger's mobility scooter, setting off the sprinkler system in the theater," Danielle said.

"Stealing and crashing Sharky's scooter, trashing the spa and destroying thousands of dollars' worth of spa products," Millie added.

"All the while hiding out in the lifeboat and even in her cabin. I hope she gets the help she needs."

"Real help. Not a luxury rehabilitation center where their idea of rehab is a shopping trip or golf outing."

"Rehab for the rich and famous. I still can't believe we saw her in the parade and finally caught her in the casino. The story would make a great tabloid headline." Danielle lifted her hands. "I can see it now... 'Bored has-been reality celebrity causes havoc on board a cruise ship while sending ship's crew on a wild goose chase.'"

"That about sums it up. Meanwhile, Bryce was filming action shots, getting ready to submit it to the producers. Andy and Cat are arriving soon." Millie glanced at her watch. "We need to head down to the bridge for our meeting. I wonder what the big announcement and meeting is about."

"Something tells me it's about Andy," Danielle said. "It's going to be so sad if he's forced to retire and leaves Siren of the Seas."

Millie could feel the tears burn the back of her eyes. "It kept me up last night, worrying about his health. I hope that's not the case. I would miss him terribly."

"We should get going. We don't want to be late."

It was a quick trek to the bridge. Millie swiped her card and followed Danielle inside. Nic was there, along with Donovan Sweeney and Dave Patterson. A pale Andy was seated nearby. He caught Millie's eye and smiled.

She made a beeline for her boss, swallowing the lump in her throat as she gave him a quick hug. "We've been worried sick about you."

"The doctors have been taking good care of me, but I'm not gonna lie...it's been a long week. I'm glad to be back."

Nic placed a light hand on Andy's shoulder. "I think I can speak for everyone in this room when I say we're equally glad to have you back with us, Andy."

"Here, here," Donovan chimed in.

"Would you like to tell everyone?" Nic asked.

Andy nodded and slowly stood. "The doctors have informed me I need to make a lifestyle change. I need more rest and less stress on the old ticker. Because of that, I'll be stepping down as the ship's cruise director, effective immediately."

Millie's lower lip trembled. "You-you're leaving us?" she whispered.

"I'm not leaving. Wild horses couldn't drag me away from Siren of the Seas. It would be like leaving my family and friends," Andy said. "I've been offered a new position."

"As the unofficial director of fun and funds," Donovan said. "Andy will still help with cruise ship activities. We've been given the green light from corporate to offer him a position, monitoring each department's spending, which will help me keep our budget aligned. We still haven't decided on an official title, but we will soon."

"So, you'll be working in two departments," Millie said.

"Yes, in both budgeting and entertainment, working alongside Donovan," Andy explained.

"Which means Siren of the Seas will be hiring a new cruise director."

Nic shook his head. "The senior officers have already met and unanimously voted on a replacement, Millie. It's you. Corporate has also already approved the request, if you're up for it."

Millie stared at Nic in disbelief. "Me?"

"It's a natural transition," Andy said. "And makes perfect sense. You're ready for that next step while I need to take a step back. It's a win-win for everyone, especially the passengers."

"The decision is yours," Donovan said.

"I..." Millie placed a hand on her chest. "Cruise director."

"More responsibility, a pay increase," Nic said. "More hours."

Millie turned to Andy. "You're sure?"

"Positive." Their eyes met. "Whether you take the position, or it goes to someone else, I'm stepping down."

"What about the assistant cruise director job? Who would take my place?"

All eyes shifted to Danielle. “Danielle could officially become your sidekick.”

“Heck yeah!” Danielle let out a whoop. “Sign me up.”

“That’s the kind of enthusiasm we need,” Donovan laughed.

“Are you sure we’re not setting ourselves up for double trouble?” Patterson teased.

“Well, Millie?” Andy placed his hand on top of Millie’s. “Are you up for the challenge?”

Millie’s eyes traveled around the bridge. Cruise director. It was an enormous responsibility. The senior officers had unanimously chosen her. They had faith she could fill Andy’s very large shoes.

She thought back to the moment she stepped on board the ship for the very first time, her life in tatters after discovering her husband Roger was cheating on her, and yet determined to start over. Her children thought she was nuts. In all honesty, there were days back in the beginning when she wondered what had ever possessed her to take the assistant cruise director position.

Now, she couldn't imagine any other life—living on a cruise ship, teaching passengers how to have fun, forging friendships. Millie had the dream life, the fairytale marriage. Being promoted to cruise director was the icing on the cake.

It would be a new adventure, a brand-new chapter. A challenge like no other she'd ever faced. Running it all—accepting the responsibility of creating passengers' dream vacations, helping *them* create memories that would last a lifetime.

Millie squared her shoulders, a wide smile spreading across her face. "I'll do it! I accept!"

The end.

The Series Continues...Book 25

Coming Soon!

Dear Reader,

I hope you enjoyed reading "Cruising Cold Turkey." Would you please take a moment to leave a review? It would mean so much. Thank you!

–Hope Callaghan

Join The Fun!

Join Hope's Cozy Newsletter to get updates on New Releases, FREE and Discounted Books, Giveaways, & More!

hopecallaghan.com

Read More by Hope

Millie's Cruise Ship Cozy Mystery Series

Hoping for a fresh start after her recent divorce, sixty something Millie Sanders, lands her dream job as the assistant cruise director onboard the "Siren of the Seas." Too bad no one told her murder is on the itinerary.

Garden Girls Cozy Mystery Series

A lonely widow finds new purpose for her life when she and her senior friends help solve a murder in their small Midwestern town.

Garden Girls - The Golden Years

The brand new spin-off series of the Garden Girls Mystery series! You'll enjoy the same fun-loving characters as they solve mysteries in the cozy town of Belhaven. Each book will focus on one of the Garden Girls as they enter their "golden years."

Lack of Luxury Series (Liz and the Garden Girls)

Green Acres meets the Golden Girls in this brand new cozy mystery spin-off series featuring Liz and the Garden Girls!

Easton Island Mystery Series

Easton Island - Looking Glass Cottage is the beginning of one woman's journey from incredible loss to finding a past she knew nothing about, including a family who both embraces and fears her and a charming island that draws her in. This inspirational series is for lovers of family sagas, mystery, and a touch of romance.

Divine Cozy Mystery Series

After relocating to the tiny town of Divine, Kansas, strange and mysterious things begin to happen to businesswoman, Jo Pepperdine and those around her.

Samantha Rite Mystery Series

Heartbroken after her recent divorce, a single mother is persuaded to book a cruise and soon finds herself caught in the middle of a deadly adventure. Will she make it out alive?

Made in Savannah Cozy Mystery Series

After the mysterious death of her mafia "made man" husband, Carlita Garlucci makes a shocking discovery. Follow the Garlucci family saga as Carlita and her daughter try to escape their NY mob ties and make a fresh start in Savannah, Georgia. They soon realize you can run but can't hide from your past.

Sweet Southern Sleuths Short Stories Series

Twin sisters with completely opposite personalities become amateur sleuths when a dead body is discovered in their recently inherited home in Misery, Mississippi.

Meet Hope Callaghan

Hope Callaghan is an American mystery author who loves to write clean fiction, especially Christian cozy mysteries. She is the author of more than 80 mystery novels in seven different series.

Born and raised in a small town in West Michigan, she now lives in Florida with her husband. She is the proud mother of 3 wonderful children.

When she's not doing the thing she loves best - writing mysteries - she enjoys cooking, traveling and reading books.

Subscribe to her cozy newsletter for a free mystery book, new releases, and giveaways at hopecallaghan.com

Amit's Lemon Cake Recipe

Ingredients:

FOR THE CAKE

3 cups all-purpose flour

½ tsp baking soda

½ tsp salt

3/4 cup Greek yogurt

1/4 cup milk

2 tablespoons grated lemon zest

2 tablespoons lemon juice

2 sticks butter, softened (1 cup)

2-¼ cups granulated sugar

3 large eggs

(You'll need two lemons)

FOR THE SYRUP

2 tablespoons water

2 tablespoons granulated sugar

2 teaspoons lemon juice

FOR THE GLAZE

1/2 cup powdered sugar

2 tablespoons lemon juice

INSTRUCTIONS

-Preheat oven to 350°F (making sure rack is in middle position.)

-Spray two 8 x 4-inch loaf pans with nonstick cooking spray.

-In a medium bowl, blend the flour, baking soda and salt. Set aside.

-In a second bowl, blend the Greek yogurt, milk, lemon zest and lemon juice. Set aside.

-Using an electric mixer with a paddle attachment or an electric mixer, cream the butter and sugar on medium speed for 3 or 4 minutes.

-Beat in one egg at a time, making sure the egg is well blended before adding the next.

-Using the lowest speed, beat in one-quarter of the flour mixture, followed by a third of the milk/yogurt mixture.

-Blend in another quarter of the flour followed by another third of the milk/yogurt mixture.

-Blend in another quarter of the flour and the remaining milk/yogurt mixture.

-Add the final remaining flour mixture and blend well.

-Pour the batter into the prepared pans and smooth top with a knife.

-Bake for 50 to 60 minutes, until a toothpick comes out clean and the top is golden brown.

-Remove from oven and place the pans on a cooling rack for ten minutes.

-Run a butter knife along the edges of the pan to loosen the cake.

-Remove the cakes and set on the cooling rack.

-Let cool for one hour.

AFTER the cakes have cooled:

-Place cakes on serving platters.

-To make the syrup:

Combine the water and sugar in a saucepan and bring to a boil. Remove from the heat and stir in the lemon juice.

Brush the syrup over the sides and tops of the cakes.

-TO make the glaze:

In a small bowl, whisk together the powdered sugar and lemon juice.

-Drizzle the glaze over the top of the cake.

-Let the cakes sit for about one hour to give the glaze time to set before serving.

Made in the USA
Columbia, SC
30 June 2025

60139993R00190